W9-AZA-401

ANGUS MACBAIN AND THE AGATE EYEGLASS

Angela Townsend

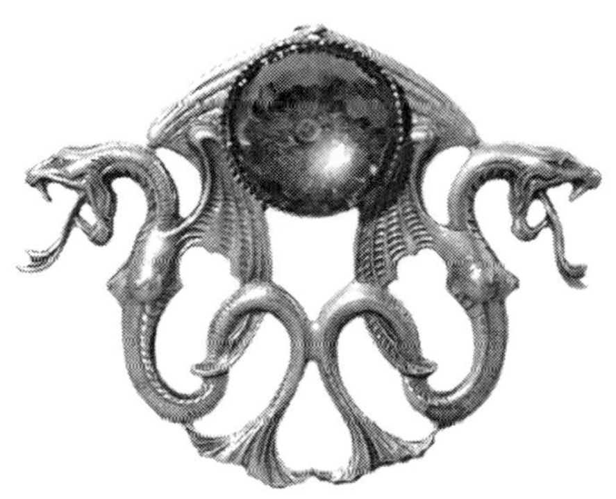

Clean Teen Publishing

Angus MacBain and The Agate Eyeglass

ISBN: 978-1-63422-040-8
Cover Design by: Marya Heiman
Typography by: Courtney Nuckels
Editing by: Cynthia Shepp

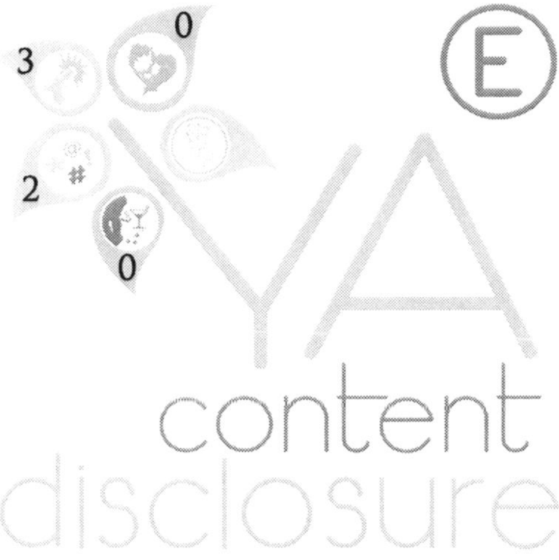

For more information about our content disclosure,
please utilize the QR code above with your smart phone or visit us at
www.CleanTeenPublishing.com.

To my family who taught me to go after my dreams
To my sons, Grant and Levi who taught me that love is endless
To Milton Datsopoulos and Diane Larsen who taught me the value of friendship
And to
Dale McGarvey
Who taught me to never give up.

1

A Parting of Ways

Fall came quickly to the island of Iona. The fields turned from green to gold and gardens blazed with the fiery hues of autumn. Bitter wind mixed with the restless sea and the blue-green waters bathed the ancient shore in an icy froth.

Thirteen-year-old Angus MacBain stood on the porch of his stone cottage, listening to the gentle clink of wind chimes. Weathered boards creaked beneath his thin socks. Shivering, he slipped on his galoshes and braced himself against a salt-stiffened breeze. A violent gust followed, knotting the wind chimes in a spinning circle. Angus reached up and held them still, studying each piece as he untangled them: bits of driftwood, rocks, and shells—treasures he'd gathered with his mother on early morning walks. Angus left the porch and hiked over a grassy knoll to the beach. Wet sand pulled at his soles as he scanned the coastline, searching for his mother.

Orla MacBain paced the shore, casting a haunted gaze

at the sea. She turned to face him with her back against the wind. “Angus,” she said, “school is starting soon, and it’s time for me to return to the ocean.” She hugged him to her. “But just for the winter months. I’ll be here to greet you when you return in the spring.”

Angus pulled away. “You’re leaving… now?”

Orla nodded and looked away. “I wish I could stay. But if I do…”

A terrible sinking sensation washed over him, like a stone cast into the sea. He didn’t want to hear what she was saying. He didn’t want her to go, to leave him again. “I know, I know.” Angus kicked at a lump of sand. “Nothing I can say or do can change anything. But why can’t I stay by myself until you come back? I’ll be fine—I promise.”

Angus’ mother knotted her long, curly hair at the nape of her neck and shook her head. “I won’t leave you alone to fend for yourself. There are still unseen dangers. You’ll be safe at school in Scotland. Ravenwood has an outstanding reputation. You’ll get an excellent education there. Vanora will show you around, and you’ll have Mr. Pegenstecher to watch over you until I return.”

“I don’t need anyone looking after me.”

Her eyes filled with sadness, and she knelt in front of him. “I know how you must feel, but I cannot deny what I am, Angus. My survival depends on it. When school is out, I’ll be back, and we’ll have all summer together. I’ll be stronger then. Until I return, you must do as I ask.”

She stood and scanned the horizon as if in a trance, fixated on the tide. Angus frowned at the ocean. It was a threat that was always present. A constant opponent in the tug-of-war over his mother. The rhythmic tide pulled at the shore, then swept back to sea, sending waves beckoning for his mother to join it, to welcome her home. Angus shook his head. It didn't make any sense. Home should be here—with him. The sea had kept her from him long enough. They had only reunited weeks ago, and now it wanted her back. Angus kicked at the sandy beach.

Orla released a heavy sigh, her shoulders sagged. "I have a long journey ahead. I'm afraid I must go."

"Now? Already!"

She glanced at Angus and then at the violet waters. "It's not by choice that I leave you. The sea is calling. I feel the pull of the tides in my veins, and on the edge of the wind there's an urgent message, warning me to go." She gripped Angus' shoulders. "Remember this—I love you above all else. My heart is with you."

Angus' eyes filled with tears. He choked them back. Orla MacBain gently tipped his chin up so that his gaze met hers. "It's only for a little while."

"A whole school year isn't a small amount of time!"

She kissed the top of Angus' head and turned suddenly. She took two steps, paused, and glanced over her shoulder to give him a weak smile. Then, she lifted the hem of her dress, ran up a steep trail leading to the cliffs, and disappeared behind a craggy shelf of rocks.

Angus' vision blurred, and his throat constricted like a drawstring pulled too tight. Every aching beat of his heart seemed to take more effort than it was worth. A dizzy numbness spread over his mind until a flood of panic snapped him out of it. He had to stop her! He needed more time. One more hour, one more minute, just one more precious second.

Angus scrambled up the rocky trail to the cliffs and searched the frothy waters below. In the distance, his mother's sleek seal body glistened in the waves. She paused, gazing at him with soft, soulful eyes, then disappeared into the depths.

Angus reached for the agate eyeglass in his pants pocket, but it was too late. His mother was gone, swallowed by the sea, taken away once again. Even so, he watched the stormy ocean for several minutes. When he was sure she was really gone, he hiked from the cliffs and along the lonely path leading home.

He thought of all the changes this year had already brought: Grandfather's death, the sad trip to Iona, the trickery of the sea hag, Prudence, posing as his aunt, his new friends Vanora and Fane, and their dangerous journey to save his mother from the evil Dragomir. And most startling of all, the knowledge that he was not an ordinary boy, but a king. A protector of two worlds and the last of his kind.

Heavy clouds drifted over the sun and he suddenly realized he'd forgotten about Vanora. Angus glanced at his watch. He'd promised to meet her at three o'clock and it was nearly three thirty! Angus raced down the footpath to Vanora's seaside cottage, rounded the corner to the picturesque bay, and found her waiting for him on a mossy boulder by the shore. A clam shovel and half-filled bucket of shellfish rested beside her.

"Sorry I'm late," he said, trying to catch his breath.

Vanora glanced up at him and smiled. "It's okay. Are you all packed for school?"

"Not yet. I'm not exactly thrilled about going."

Vanora nodded and fingered a small, white shell in the palm of her hand. "I know what you mean. I don't look forward to boarding school either. But we'll be back here for summer before you know it."

"At least you'll get to see your dad during the holidays. My mom returned to the sea again. She insisted I leave Iona for a proper education." Angus picked up a rock and hurled it into the ocean. "I hate school."

The stone skipped across the foamy surface, flew into the air, and bounced off something in the water.

Vanora lowered her voice. "What was that?"

Angus frowned and narrowed his eyes. "I don't know…"

A dark shape undulated through the breakers, swimming closer. Angus' heart jumped. Maybe his mother had returned. He peered into the foamy waves and sucked in his breath. The top of a slimy head burst from the water. A sludgy smile formed on the green face, its goopy eyes narrowed.

The shell slipped from Vanora's trembling hand. "Is that who I think it is?"

Angus stared at the monster. Fear stuck in his throat like paste, gripping his tongue, fusing his jaw shut. The face, although distorted, looked all too familiar. Prudence—the horrible sea hag that had posed as his aunt!

Angus latched onto Vanora's arm. "Come on, let's get out of here!"

Vanora grabbed her clamming trowel. "I thought we were rid of that sea hag for good."

"So did I."

They peered over their shoulders as they ran, watching as the sea hag raced to shore and dove under the sand. The hag traveled like a lightning bolt under the wet earth, forming a huge tunnel behind her. Just as they reached the grass, Angus' foot slipped on the sod. He lost his balance and pitched forward.

The hag exploded from the sand, opened her jaws wide, and bit into his ankle. Two rows of needle-like teeth sunk into his flesh, and Angus screamed.

With his free leg, he kicked at her head. Green slime flew in all directions.

The sea hag released his foot, lunged forward, and gripped his legs with loops of slithery seaweed. She flipped him onto his stomach, dragging him toward the tunnel.

Vanora leaped forward and grabbed Angus' hands, but the hag wrenched him free.

Angus clawed at the sand in savage strokes, trying to stop from being pulled inside, but the sea hag yanked even harder, forcing him into the mucky passageway.

Vanora's screams echoed in Angus' ears. He caught one last glimpse of her panic-stricken eyes as he was pulled away, disappearing into the sand tunnel.

2

The Casting of a Curse

Sticky ropes of seaweed pulled Angus faster and faster through the collapsing sand tunnel. Angus twisted savagely to free himself, but the grip only tightened until it cocooned around him. The stink of rotten fish filled his nostrils and icy froth washed up his pant legs as the sea hag dragged him past the tide line.

A jarring clunk echoed into the darkness, and the grasp on his ankles released. The tip of a shovel pierced the tunnel, and Angus spotted Vanora's pink tennis shoes.

She crouched to help him out. "Are you all right?"

He seized Vanora's hand as he spit out chunks of sand and seaweed. "I think so."

Angus stared at the motionless figure that had attacked him. He wanted to run at her and give her a swift kick, but instead hobbled farther up the beach, spitting out specks of sand stuck in his teeth. A jab of pain in his foot forced him to stop. He glanced over his shoulder again to make sure they weren't being followed and struggled to take another step.

"My ankle's killing me." He grimaced and pointed behind him, at the unmoving blob in the sand. "But the farther we get from that thing, the better. Let's go!"

"I conked her pretty hard with my clamming shovel. I don't think she'll be coming after anyone." Vanora's eyes danced. "I can't wait to show my dad that thing. I'm sure he's never documented a sea hag before! Just think of the press he'll get. Maybe he'll even be on the nightly news!"

"Just as long as he doesn't get too close. Otherwise it will be a gory broadcast."

Angus balanced on one leg, kicked off his mangled shoe, and pulled his sock down to examine the angry wound.

"Ouch," Vanora said. "Better get some salve on it right away. Can you make it to the cottage?" She scrunched up her nose. "No telling what diseases that hag's got. Hope you've had all your shots. An infection could cause gangrene, which can kill you."

Angus' stomach twisted. The last thing he wanted was to get sick with something dreadful.

Vanora grimaced. "Sometimes amputation is the only option a person has left for an infected wound. In fact, I know a man that was bitten by a black mamba and his skin...."

Angus glanced at his ankle. "Great. As if I don't already have enough to worry about. All I can think of is my mother swimming around in the same ocean with horrible monsters."

Vanora sighed. "I doubt your mom's anywhere near

here. Selkies are fast swimmers. That's why most people never see them."

Angus bit his lower lip. "I hope you're right."

The world tilted beneath Angus' feet, pain seared into his temples. "Whoa." He stretched out his hands to keep his balance.

Vanora grabbed his arm. "What's the matter?"

A faint whisper hissed in his ears. *You must find what's missing... the ancient library.* The voice was strange, yet familiar. The dizziness lifted from his head. "Fane's trying to communicate with me, but he sounds strange. His voice is so weak."

Angus concentrated hard, clamping his eyes shut, but no more messages came from Fane.

Vanora frowned. "What did he say?"

Angus shook his head. "I'm not sure. Something about finding what's missing and an ancient library. He sounds like he's sick or something." Angus' stomach churned again. "I have to sit down."

"We're almost to the house. Just a couple more steps."

Angus hobbled up the path to the front porch of Vanora's cottage. Each step sent a sharp stab of pain into his foot.

"Let's get you inside." Vanora pushed open the door. "Dad! Hey, Dad! We need help."

Angus expected Mr. Pegenstecher's welcoming voice or friendly smile, but no answer came. Vanora gave Angus a concerned look. "I know he's around here somewhere. I just left him not that long ago to get some clams for dinner." She pointed to a wooden bench near the door. "Have a seat while I search for him."

Angus sat down and studied the inside of the cottage, filled with artifacts from Mr. Pegenstecher's unusual occupation, cryptozoology. Each wall contained a mystery. Detailed models of trolls, Nessie, Bigfoot, and scores of other cryptids crowded every corner. Shelves brimmed with hundreds of plaster casts of tiny to giant footprints, skulls, fossils and furred fish.

Angus spotted something on Mr. Pegenstecher's desk. "Look. There's a note!"

"Where?"

Angus pointed to a piece of rumpled paper resting on a stack of books. Vanora rushed over and picked up the parchment by one edge. A green liquid dripped from the note onto the desk. She held the letter at arm's length. "Phew! It's soaking wet and stinks like seaweed. I can't read a word of what it says."

"Prudence!" Angus scowled. "She must have been here first before she attacked us on the beach."

Vanora's eyes flew open. She bit her lower lip. "You... you don't think she did something to him, do you?"

Angus stared at the dripping paper in Vanora's hand and his stomach knotted. "I don't know. Maybe he went somewhere."

Vanora pointed to a pair of loafers. "Not without his shoes. It's his only pair."

"And his laptop." Angus nodded to a small computer resting on a chair near the front door. Angus' heart grew cold. Mr. Pegenstecher never went anywhere without his laptop.

Vanora swept through the tiny cottage again, shouting for her father, her voice rising in pitch with each passing moment. She stopped and stood in front of Angus. Her face filled with worry. "Something isn't right. You can't kidnap a full grown man without being spotted."

Vanora paced back and forth before striding to the other side of the room. She shuffled through her father's untidy desk, found nothing and slumped into his computer chair. Vanora immediately jumped to her feet, letting out a high-pitched shriek.

Angus nearly leapt out of his skin. "What's the matter?"

Vanora's eyes went wide. She turned slowly and pointed a shaky finger at the empty chair. "I just sat on someone's lap."

"What are you talking about?"

"I mean, there's someone sitting in that chair!"

Angus sighed. "This was no time for joking around. I think you need a new prescription for your glasses."

"See for yourself." Vanora patted the chair. "Feel right there. A perfect set of legs."

Angus hobbled closer, cautiously leaned forward, and touched the seat. Beneath his fingertips, he felt a warm pair of legs covered in a fleece material. Angus jerked his hand back.

Vanora crossed her arms. "See, I told you."

"Who's there?" Angus demanded, trying to muster his scariest sounding voice. When he got no reply, an idea came to him. He pulled out the agate eyeglass from his pocket. It never worked like an eyeglass should, although it did serve as a telescope for a few moments. It only showed events that had just taken place—an instrument used for looking into the recent past. It was ornamented with Celtic knotwork and had a long tunneling scope that could collapse into a pocket-sized instrument.

Angus peered around the room; the eyeglass showed nothing. Then, a moment later, he spotted Prudence bent over and sloshing toward Mr. Pegenstecher's desk. Her long, black dress crawled with sand crabs clicking their claws. What used to be her hair was now tentacles oozing with slime. Angus took the eyeglass away from his eye just to be sure what he was seeing was really from the past. The image of the sea hag vanished.

"What did you see?" Vanora asked eagerly.

"Just as I suspected. Prudence was here." Angus put the eyeglass back to his eye and watched as Mr. Pegenstecher stood up from his chair, his mouth agape. With a wave of her hand, the sea hag shoved him back into his seat. He sat, wide-eyed and unable to speak or move, while Prudence muttered some kind of spell.

"She's put a curse on him," Angus said. "And it's..." He paused for a moment watching through the eyeglass as Mr. Pegenstecher became more and more invisible. "An invisibility curse!"

Prudence snatched a sheet of paper with a crustacean-like hand. She dipped a long twisted fingernail into the inkwell and started to scrawl out a message. Angus peered over the hag's shoulder as she wrote and read the words aloud.

I took the talisman that keeps that meddling old wizard alive between worlds. Release Lord Dragomir, or you'll never see the wizard or the stupid human alive again.

Vanora's eyes filled with tears. "Oh no. My poor dad."

Angus' face grew hot. "I'll never release Dragomir—never! And don't worry, we'll find a way to free your dad and Fane." Angus clutched his fists. "I'll make her give back whatever she's stolen from us and take that curse off your dad."

Vanora tossed Angus an ace bandage and some ointment. "Here. Put this on your ankle. We gotta get back to the shore before the sea hag gets away! I'm heading down to the beach now. Catch up when you can."

"Wait for me!"

Vanora ignored him and rushed out the door.

Angus slapped on the salve, wrapped his ankle, and scrambled out the door. Vanora was far ahead of him by the time he reached the shoreline. Angus tried to run faster, but the pain in his ankle wouldn't allow it. When he finally caught up to her, she was standing next to the spot where the sea hag had once been.

"She's gone," Vanora said, her voice cracking. She turned and looked at Angus, her face streaked with tears. "Now what are we going to do?"

Angus scanned the stormy waters. "Fane said something about an ancient library. Is there one on Iona?"

Vanora thought for a moment. "No, not that I know of."

"What about the museum?"

Vanora shook her head.

Angus couldn't think of where a library could be. Iona was such a small island. Just a few houses, a couple of bed and breakfasts, and of course, the beautiful Iona Abbey.

"Do you think there would be anything about it in your grandfather's book?" Vanora asked.

Angus frowned. "I don't remember anything about a library, but let's go check it out."

By the time they reached Angus' house, the sun appeared to have sunk halfway into the sea. Angus hurried up the steps and held the door open for Vanora as they slipped inside. The once cold and uninviting cottage now brimmed with his mother's things, interesting objects from the deep: ornate shells, trinkets whittled from bones, Japanese glass floats in faded blues and greens, and long shanks of seaweed drying near the hearth.

Vanora nervously fingered a piece of driftwood carved into the shape of a seal. "Can you try to contact Fane again to see if he knows how to help my father?"

Angus nodded. "I can try, but like I said, he didn't sound good. Something is really wrong." He sat on a chair fashioned from weathered whalebone near a table carved from the hull of a shipwreck. Angus rested his feet on a lavish chest filled with sunken treasures his mother had salvaged from the wreckage.

Angus clamped his eyes shut. He pictured the kindly old man and concentrated hard, but no words came to him. *Fane, please talk to me. We need your help, Prudence is back, and she did something to Vanora's dad. He's invisible and doesn't respond when we talk to him.* Angus waited several seconds then tried again. *Tell me what to do. Please!*

Nothing.

Angus frowned. "I'm sorry, he's not saying anything. I'm worried about Fane; it's strange that he's not speaking to me. Telepathically, I mean. I hope he's okay."

"Remember what the note said?" Vanora asked.

"Prudence said she took the thing that keeps Fane alive between the two worlds. Think about it. He's centuries old in our world, but there really isn't any time in his. He doesn't age there." Vanora's voice dropped. "There must be an object here on Iona that keeps him from rapidly aging and turning into dust. He could be dying, Angus."

Angus jumped to his feet. "We have to find out what it is and get it back. We have to save him, and we need him to help your dad."

Vanora frowned. "Problem is, Prudence could have taken it anywhere, or even destroyed it by now."

A surge of fear shot through Angus. "Hopefully all the answers are in the library—if we can find it." Angus glanced up the staircase. "Come on. Let's look in my grandfather's book."

They clambered upstairs to Angus' bedroom. He threw back the trunk lid that held his grandfather's things and sifted through it until he found the volume Duncan MacBain had made for him. He ran his hand over the cover, and then flipped it open, thumbing through the pages.

Angus sat back on his heels. "There's nothing in here about a library. Not one word."

Vanora held out her hand. "Do you mind if I take a look?"

Angus handed her the book and shuffled through the rest of the contents in the trunk.

"Here!" Vanora exclaimed, pointing to a faded page. "Listen to this. It's a section about the secret halls of Staffa." She flipped to the next page. "All are welcome in the great Hall of Learning and Reference. That could be the library Fane's talking about, right?"

"Yes!" Angus scrambled to his feet. "That means we'll have to make a trip to the island and use the entrance inside Fingal's Cave again. But how will we get there?"

Vanora grinned. "We have my father's rowboat. And while we're in the library, I bet we can also find a spell to release my dad!"

Angus remembered the weather-beaten, old boat resting on the beach and shuddered. "We can't get to Staffa in that old thing. It's too dangerous."

"Of course not."

Angus shook his head. "I'm confused. You just said..."

"I know what I said, but I didn't mean we'd take the boat all the way." Vanora's eyes danced as she pointed to a metal gong resting inside the trunk under a stack of books. "We could use that to summon The Black Dragon, and Dad's old boat should get us out just far enough to meet Captain Lee's ship."

Angus smiled, remembering how Captain Lee and his ship, the Black Dragon, had helped them before. He pulled out the gong with two metal strikers attached to the side. "Let's go!"

3

A Ride to Fingal's Cave

ngus studied the boat resting on the beach and raised an eyebrow. "Does this thing leak?"

"Only a little."

Angus pushed the boat into the water and climbed in. "Er… what do you mean only a little?"

"Enough to get your feet wet." Vanora settled into her seat. "If we hurry and get a couple miles out, I bet we'll find Captain Lee before it sinks."

"Sinks? Are you kidding me?"

Vanora flung a life preserver at Angus. "If you'd quit talking and row a little faster, we wouldn't have to worry."

Angus caught the vest with one hand. "Sheesh, you're a bit touchy today."

Vanora's eyes welled up with tears. "Well, shouldn't I be? My dad's frozen and invisible."

"You're right. I'm sorry."

Vanora hung her head. "Me too. I didn't mean to be so snappy."

Angus pulled hard on the oars, traveling swiftly through the choppy waters. "I don't blame you for being upset. I really like your dad, and I'm worried, too."

Vanora's bottom lip trembled. "He's all I have—I mean, besides you."

Angus rested the oars across his lap. "It's going to be okay. We just have to figure out how to undo the curse, and then everything will be back to normal… or as normal as things get around here. Now hand me the gong."

Vanora pulled the instrument from the sack and gave it to him. "Looks like it comes with a tin whistle."

Angus studied the strikers fixed to the side. "You know, you're right. I thought it was just an extra striker. There's something written on it." Angus squinted to read the writing. "Equine Ocean Liner—emergency travel only."

Vanora lifted a pink sandal. "You better hurry, Angus. My shoes are getting soaked."

Angus tucked the whistle into his pocket and struck the gong.

The sound vibrated far out to sea. They waited, gazing in all directions, but no boat emerged. The water rose higher inside the boat. It seeped through his shoelaces. His socks were soaked. Angus tried scooping out the water with his hands, but it was coming too fast. To make matters worse, Angus' ankle felt like it was on fire.

"We have to figure out where all the water is coming in at." Angus rubbed his foot.

"There!" Vanora pointed to a hole under Angus' seat. "We need to plug it with something—quick!"

Angus ripped a piece off the bottom of his T-shirt,

wadded it up, and shoved it inside the hole. The material held for only a moment before it popped out and water gushed in.

Vanora tightened her life vest. "We better try to return to the shore. Hope we can make it before it goes under."

"Me too! Better get ready to swim."

Angus dipped the oars into the water and rowed hard back the way they came.

"Wait!" Vanora cried. "I see something!"

Sure enough, a cloud of mist was rising in the west.

Across the horizon, Angus spotted the flash of transparent sails and the outline of an enormous ship.

Vanora stood and waved her arms. The rowboat rocked dangerously. The vessel drew closer. She sat down. "It certainly isn't Captain Lee's ship. It's a pirate ship, and the sails look… bloody." Vanora lowered her arms and stared at Angus, her eyes wide. "Was that the same gong Fane used when he summoned the Black Dragon?"

Angus shook his head. "No, this is a different one." He picked up the instrument. "There's a name written on it." Angus turned the gong over. "H. W. Ruskin."

Vanora flinched. "Ruskin? Are you sure?"

Angus rubbed at the metal and then took another look. "Yep. That's what it says."

Vanora clutched Angus' arm. "The Black Mary!"

"The Black who?" Angus repeated.

"Henry Ruskin was captain of the Black Mary. He traveled the Orient in the 1300s until he and his whole crew were stricken with the black plague. Every port the captain came to turned him away. No one wanted a plague-ridden ship in their bay. So, eventually they ran out of provisions, and all on board died. It sails the seas nonstop, searching for more souls to capture to man the ship."

Angus jerked his head toward the ship, closing in at a hundred yards. "Are you saying… that's a ghost ship?"

Vanora nodded. "And worse yet, legend has it the ship is a symbol of doom and spells disaster to all who come in contact with her."

"Are you serious? How do you know this?"

"Because… remember when we were in the Hall of Dargis? And we barely escaped those rat things?"

Angus nodded. "How could I forget?"

"Fane told us the Dargis were the cause of the black plague in the dark times. They purposely passed their vermin to regular rats, who were aboard a cargo ship docked at Staffa. As soon as we got back to Iona, my curiosity got the best of me. After some research I found the name of the ship. The Black Mary. I knew it had to be the right one when I read about the crew getting sick and all."

Water rose past Vanora's ankles. "We need to do something—quick."

The ship sailed closer with an eerie, unnatural glow. The enormous vessel raised a flag with a hooded skeleton holding a plague lantern. Its three giant masts dripped with seaweed, crusty barnacles, and crawled with sea creatures, as if it had just risen from the bottom of the ocean. The ship's bell clanged three times, echoing forlornly out to sea. The ship suddenly sped up, slicing through the water, cannons raised. The prow of the ship resembled the nose of a shark, and featured a carved figurehead of a horned beast with cloven hooves.

"It's coming right at us!" Vanora screamed.

Angus pulled hard on the oars, but more water seeped inside the boat. He leaned forward, scooping water with his hands. The whistle slipped from his pocket; he caught it just in time.

"Hey," Angus said. "Maybe this will call it off."

Vanora paled. "What if it doesn't? What if it does the opposite? Like sink us?

"What choice do we have? It's worth a shot, isn't it?"

Vanora glanced at the approaching ship and then nodded quickly.

He put the whistle to his lips and blew hard. A shrill alarm erupted. The waters boiled beneath them, jostling the boat like a cork. Angus peered over the side.

A white flash of something undulated just under the surface.

"Look," Angus said.

Vanora's mouth hung open. "Oh my gosh, please tell me that's not a shark!"

Angus stared overboard, eyes wide and chest so tight he could hardly breathe. He caught a glimpse of something else there—something with a long, flowing mane.

"No—wait—it's a…"

"It's a sea stallion!" Vanora yelled.

"Didn't Fane say they'd take you for a ride and then drown you?"

"That was a kelpie—this is a different breed."

"I hope you're right."

"I know I am. My father has tons of books on them.

These horses are cousins to the Loch Ness Monster. Except they have hooves and can travel on top of the water, of course." Vanora paused. "Look—it's coming to the surface!"

The horse burst from the depths and rose until it was trotting on the tips of the waves, its golden hooves in constant motion as it expelled the water from its silver mane with a fling of its head. The stallion's blue eyes blazed. It maneuvered itself to stand sideways to the boat, sinking downward, treading water so its back was easily mountable.

The ship loomed over them.

Angus slipped onto the horse's back, ignoring the nagging pain in his ankle. He grabbed a handful of silver mane with one hand and extended the other. "Hurry, jump on!" Vanora grabbed Angus' hand, and he pulled her effortlessly onto the horse.

4

King of the Deep

The stallion raced across the waves, leaving the ghost ship and their sinking rowboat behind. The bitter wind made Angus' eyes and nose water. He leaned forward and grabbed the horse's neck, while Vanora wrapped her arms tight around his middle.

"Ouch! Loosen your grip, boa constrictor."

"I'm sorry, but it's hard to stay on."

Vanora unclasped her arms enough to allow Angus to inhale a deep breath of salty sea air. Within moments, wisps of fog cleared, and the rocky outcropping of the uninhabited island of Staffa came into view. On the south end stood the large, arched entrance into Fingal's Cave, or Uamh-Binn, the Cave of Melody. The water around the gaping grotto with narrow slippery ledges was bottomless and black. Hidden deep within the cave's protective walls, tucked behind accordion-like folds of volcanic rock, stood the doorway into the Hall of Kings. The cave's naturally domed roof and the rush of entering waves created haunting melodies, which soothed the terrible sea monster guarding the secret entry.

Angus' stomach tightened. He dreaded the thought of going back inside the dark and dangerous halls without Fane to guide them through the maze of monsters and treacherous terrain. Worse yet, Angus didn't have his sword and shield to protect them. His mother had locked them away, hidden them in a safe place so he could focus on returning to school. He hadn't planned on a new adventure so soon; otherwise, he would have been more prepared, and he would have asked for his weapons before his mother left.

Angus thought about how disappointed his mother would be that instead of school he was risking his life again. What if he never returned? Would she ever know what happened to him? Angus steadied himself. He didn't have time to dwell on such things now. His focus had to be on the journey ahead—no matter how hard it might be.

The horse leapt from the water and clambered onto the rocky shore, its hooves scrabbling for traction on the slick surface. Vanora lost her grip and slid off the stallion's back, dragging Angus to the ground with her. He landed with a thud on the rocks, just barely missing Vanora.

"Ouch!" Angus grabbed his wounded ankle.

"Sorry, I couldn't hold on any longer."

He got to his feet. "Remind me to take out health insurance the next time we go on an adventure."

Vanora winced and rubbed the palms of her hands on her shorts. "Yeah, I will. It probably would be a good idea. Maybe life insurance would be a better idea. At least we could leave our loved ones something besides bloody remains."

Angus groaned. "You always have to take it to another level, don't you?"

"Well it's true, isn't it? We do risk our lives."

Angus raised an eyebrow. "I know, but you could have left out the bloody body parts." He grabbed hold of Vanora's arm and helped her to her feet. For a second, she had trouble getting her footing on the algae-covered rocks.

"Gross, everything is covered in slime."

"It's just seaweed," Angus said. "Watch your step."

The sea stallion trotted on the rocks, not minding the slippery surface. The horse flipped its head, displacing bits of salt and ocean water from its luscious mane. Angus turned and reached to stroke the horse's sleek neck. But before he could touch it, the animal wheeled, then bolted onto the surface of the water. It galloped hard across the stormy waves, kicking up its heels and sinking beneath the cresting whitecaps. It raced away with ease until it faded away under an orange sunset.

"Man, I wish I had my camera," Vanora said.

"I wish you did, too. That horse is so cool. Did you see the way it ran off so fast? I wish I could be that graceful. Seems like all I do is trip over my own feet."

"I wonder where it goes."

"Someplace golden and beautiful in the middle of the sea, I would guess."

They took off their life vests and tossed them to the ground. Vanora sighed and pushed her glitter-framed glasses higher onto her nose. She nodded toward Fingal's

Cave. "How are we going to open the doorway? Last time we used the harp, but Fane tossed it to that creepy sea monster, Ferock, remember?"

"How can I forget?" Angus eyed the waters, which dropped off from the shore into the bottomless ocean. His throat grew tight. The harp was no doubt in Ferock's sea cave. "Guess I'll have to dive for it."

Vanora's pale eyes widened. "Angus, you can't! It's too dangerous. Ferock will tear you to pieces! There'll be bloody chunks floating everywhere. What if he only tears off your legs and you can't swim to the surface before he eats you?"

Angus sighed. "You know—you're not making things any easier for me."

Vanora planted her hands on her hips. "What do you want me to do—let you get yourself killed?"

"Whatever makes you feel better—I've been doing a pretty good job of protecting us both, in case you hadn't noticed."

"It's not like I've been standing around doing nothing and…"

"Okay, so we make a great team—as long as you don't go all gory on me."

"Sometimes I just can't help myself." Vanora stuck her nose in the air.

Angus rolled his eyes. "Believe me, I've noticed."

"So I get a little graphic at times—what's the big deal?"

Angus took the agate eyeglass from his pocket, knelt, and put the tip into the water.

"What do you see?" Vanora asked.

"Just a second." Angus adjusted the lens. Everything

looked so blurry under the water.

"Well?" Vanora asked again. "Do you see anything?"

Angus squinted to get a better look. More weeds floated past.

"Do you see anything or not?"

"Yes," Angus replied. "A sign that says 'www.willyoupleaseshutup.com'."

"Very funny. I'll just stand here and not say a word the whole time and let you figure out everything on your own."

Angus ignored her and strained to see through the murky, churning water. When it cleared, a vision of the massive sea monster, roughly the size of a school bus, appeared from an undersea cavern. Angus' heart skipped as the colossal beast swam closer. His throat tightened as he remembered the last encounter he'd had with the horrible sea monster, when it tried to drag Vanora into the ocean.

Long, green tentacles with barbed hooks and claws at their ends propelled Ferock's massive girth through the depths. Angus steadied himself. Was the beast really there or was he watching something that had already happened? It was hard to tell with the eyeglass. No matter whether he was seeing the past or the present, Angus' hand shook, and the vision blurred. He steadied himself, resisting the urge to jerk the eyeglass from the water as the enormous monster glided past.

The sea monster suddenly paused, its long arms dancing in the water. Ferock charged ahead without warning, bolting into deeper waters. Angus' heart raced. What was he after? Angus hoped it wasn't the beautiful sea stallion that had brought them here. Whatever it was would soon be prey—something Ferock would rip to shreds.

Long stalks of sea kelp and underwater vegetation floated into Angus' line of vision. He reached into the water and tried to wave it away. When the seaweed and sludge drifted past, the waters cleared, and Angus nearly dropped his eyeglass when he saw the reason for Ferock's haste.

A tour boat, probably the last of the season, filled with unsuspecting passengers, idled near Fingal's Cave. Tourists came all summer to see the "Cave of Melody" because of the haunting sounds produced by the water and the interior of the cave. But because of the choppy waters and chilly temperatures there weren't many visitors in the fall. So whatever Angus saw had to have happened earlier in the year.

Angus continued to watch Ferock stalk the boat. He didn't want to, but he couldn't drag his eyes away from it.

Ferock slowed as he approached the helpless vessel, surveying his potential kill, and floated near the hull, treading water, his serpent-like tentacles twirling. The monster extended a long arm with barbed hooks to slice the bottom of the boat, when a passenger leaned overboard, peering into the water.

The man, who looked a lot like a short, dark, Italian man from one of Angus' favorite Nintendo games, wore a long lens camera around his neck. While the other passengers were paying attention to the tour guide, the man was leaning farther and farther over the edge of the boat. The tourist raised his camera and seemed to be studying the dark shadow in the water.

Ferock swam slowly toward the tour boat, watching those on board with his enormous, black eyes. Someone tossed a can overboard, and the mollusk's massive limbs twisted in fury at the intrusion into his territory. Air holes on the inner side of Ferock's tentacles dilated wide. The monster's mouth, a beak sharp as a pair of shears, opened and snapped shut. Ferock's tongue, a horned thing that seemed to have a life of its own, quivered out of his terrible mouth. The twelve-ton monster changed from a livid gray to bright, reddish-brown.

The man with the camera leaned overboard to retrieve the can, and Ferock struck quickly, whipping out a tentacle and seizing the man. More tentacles wrapped around the man's throat and across his mouth, and then Ferock jerked him out of the boat, his hooks burying into the man's flesh. The man flailed violently as he tried to pull the tentacle free, never able to scream or call attention to himself before slipping away into the sea.

Angus held his breath, waiting for the man to resurface, but all he saw in the water was a cloud of black ink and a pool of something that looked like blood. Angus' hand shook as he kept the eyeglass pointed at the horrible sight. The ship, not noticing its missing passenger, suddenly sped away just as Ferock reappeared to strike again.

In a rage, Ferock filled the waters with a flurry of more ink, and Angus feared he would charge after the boat. But, the sea monster only sulked back down into the depths and disappeared inside his cave.

Angus' pulse pounded in his ears. With shaking hands, he jerked the eyeglass from the sea and shook droplets of water from his face and hair. Swiping a damp sleeve across his forehead, he clamped his eyes shut for a moment, hoping that when he opened them it would have all been some sort of horrific dream.

Vanora rested on a rock behind him. "I hate to ask, in case you freak out and tell me I'm being too noisy again, but what did you see?"

Angus shuddered. He clutched his stomach. The whole scene had made him sick. His ankle throbbed all the more, and for a few moments he couldn't think straight. It was all too terrible.

Vanora came to his side and lightly tapped his shoulder. "What is it, Angus? What did you see?"

He shook his head. "It was… I don't think you want to know."

"Tell me. What happened?"

Beads of sweat dotted Angus' upper lip. "I think I just saw someone die."

"What!"

"There was a man on a tour boat and he was leaning over the side and then Ferock snatched him and probably—"Angus swallowed hard—"ate him."

"Oh my gosh, that's horrible! Are you sure? Maybe he got away. Should we try to help him?"

Angus shook his head. "I don't think he made it. I saw blood."

"Didn't anyone else notice? Did they try to help?"

Angus plowed his hands through his hair. "No, everyone was busy with the tour. They were all looking at Fingal's Cave when Ferock snuck up and snatched the poor guy. He must have been traveling alone. He looked like a professional photographer or something, not just a common tourist. He had a huge camera with a long lens."

"Ugh, that's horrible. I wonder if Ferock paralyzed him with venom before he ripped him apart to eat him, or if—"

"What is it with you?" he snapped. "Don't you ever stop?"

"Well, makes you wonder, doesn't it? What his last moments were like, and—"

"No, it doesn't! And honestly, I'd like to forget it, not analyze it. Especially since I have to dive into the water with that creepy thing."

"I told you not to—but, of course, you won't listen to reason. If you dive in there, you could end up dead, too."

"What choice do I have? We have to get inside, and the only way is with the harp, right?"

Vanora studied the opening and sighed. "I guess you're right. Look, I'm sorry for being so graphic, but I may have already lost my dad, and I don't want to lose you, too. I just want to make sure you're aware of the danger."

Angus peered into the water. "Believe me, I know how dangerous it is. I've done this before, remember? Ferock has a cave not far from the surface. If I remember right, it's only about twenty feet, at most. Last time I was there, I saw where he stashes his loot. That's gotta be where he keeps the harp. We'll have to figure out a way to draw him out, distract him, so I can get it."

"Ferock will kill you! You know how he loves that harp."

Angus kicked off his shoes and stared into the emerald green water. "It's the only way. If we don't get it we will never get inside and Fane and your father will…" Angus allowed the thought to hang in the air for a moment.

Vanora looked away. Angus handed her the whistle from his pocket. "Listen, I want you to play a tune, or sing, or even dance a jig if you have to—anything to keep him distracted. Stay far enough from the ledge so he doesn't grab you like last time."

"Don't remind me. I still have the scars." Vanora paused. "What happens if it summons the water horse again?"

"It won't. If you look at the fine print on the side it says it's only good for one use."

"Glad you are so sure about that, Angus."

"Well what else should I do? Think the worst? If I do that then I will never get anything done." Angus peeled off his T-shirt and tossed it on top of his shoes. "Go ahead and start playing. Don't stop, no matter what. Keep it up until I surface with the harp."

"What should I play?"

Angus shrugged. "Play Twinkle, Twinkle Little Star—anything."

Vanora put the whistle to her trembling lips and blew. A few squeaks and high-pitched notes came out. She pulled the instrument from her mouth and winced. "Wow, I really suck at this."

Angus waved her on. "Who cares—just keep playing! It's not like it's an audition or anything!"

"But I've never been good at wind instruments, only strings!"

"Come on!"

"Okay, but I'm just saying." Vanora returned the

whistle to her lips and played as loud and fast as she could. Angus winced and covered his ears.

The waters bubbled. Vanora continued to play, taking several steps back from the ledge.

Angus spotted a saucer-like eye just below the surface. "There he is," he whispered. "He's watching. Keep playing—just don't stop!"

Vanora blew louder, squeaking out a terrible tune that made Angus' ears ache.

"What are you trying to do—distract him or make him go nuts and kill us?"

Vanora glared at Angus. "I told you! What do you expect? I'm nervous. You want me to keep playing or what?"

"I'm sorry. Just try to relax a little so you don't sound so bad."

She put the whistle to her lips, closed her eyes, and played again. This time a soft tune echoed gently from the walls and into the dark waters.

A long tentacle slithered onto shore and wove over the rocky ledge; the slimy claw at the end groped the rocks as if searching for the source of the sound. Vanora crept farther from its reach and continued to play. Ferock's eyes remained fixed on her, entranced by the sounds of the whistle.

Angus slipped into the water and swam gently around the sea monster's massive frame. Any thrashing movements and Ferock would turn and attack him. After pulling in a deep breath, Angus sank into the murky depths.

A few feet ahead, a misty light marked the entrance

into the sea monster's den. He swam hard toward the light. Something long and slimy slithered around his sore ankle. Ferock had him! He twisted around to face the beast.

If he was quick he might be able to get away before the sea monster could take hold. He yanked his foot. To Angus' surprise it came free. If he hadn't been underwater and holding his breath, he would've laughed. It was just a mammoth hunk of seaweed that had become twisted in the bandage on his ankle. Angus flung the slimy vine off his foot. The bandage slid off with it.

He continued onward, ignoring the pain in his ankle and the burn in his lungs. Angus ducked into Ferock's cave and rose into an air pocket. He filled his aching lungs with stagnant but soothing oxygen, and he treaded water a moment while he rested. Sucking in a breath, he dove again and swam deep into the sea cave.

Bones littered the floor—some of them chewed clean, others covered in clumps of rotting flesh. Angus spotted the harp resting on a pile of gold doubloons, silver chalices, and precious gemstones. He snatched it and kicked toward the entrance, pausing at the air pocket to fill his lungs again.

He'd have to maneuver around Ferock and surface outside of Fingal's Cave in order to have time to scramble onto shore unnoticed. His pulse quickened as he pumped his legs like a frog, swimming upward until Ferock's long tentacles came into view. The water boiled and churned around the sea monster. Angus moved cautiously around the colossal beast and out the cave entrance, surfacing where they'd landed with the horse. He rested against the waist-high shoreline and greedily gulped air into his starved lungs. Angus carefully placed the harp on top of the rock. He held onto the slippery sides of the boulder. Angus pulled himself up, but his foot slipped and he fell back into the water. He grabbed a hold again, this time wedging his fingers into a crack, and started to hoist himself up.

Plunk! A string near the top of the instrument snapped.

Angus froze.

Vanora stopped playing and jumped to her feet. “Look out!”

The water inside the cave exploded, sending a giant tsunami toward him.

Angus gripped an algae-covered rock, scrambling halfway out of the water, but the current sucked at his body and wrenched him back into the ocean.

Ferock streaked after him, cutting through the sea like a blade before plunging deep into the agitated waters to snake underneath him. Angus jerked as cold, mucous-coated skin brushed the bottoms of his bare feet. Adrenaline ignited his arms and legs. He kicked savagely to reach the shore again. Just two more strokes and he’d be there.

Ferock’s massive head burst from the deep. The sea monster’s eyes rolled back in their sockets as the beast swung his giant jaws open. Angus gaped into the hellacious cavity, big enough to swallow a whale. Rotting bits of flesh and ooze dangled from rows of twelve-inch fangs.

A terrible stench overpowered his senses. Bile rose in Angus’ throat, and he struggled to breathe. His eyes watcred so badly he couldn't see the sea monster anymore—all he could hear was Vanora's terrified screams. They penetrated deep inside his eardrums as he stared death in the face.

Ferock lunged and sucked Angus into his gaping gullet.

5

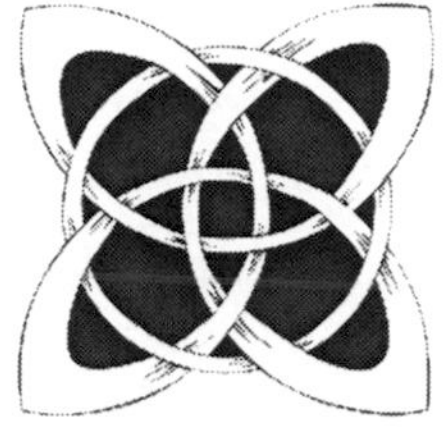

The Seeing

Angus grabbed onto a broken fang at the back of Ferock's mouth just before going down the sea monster's piano-sized throat. His feet dangled dangerously over the gaping black hole. A sickening heat rose from the sea monster's belly, mixed with the scent of fish and fresh blood. Sweat beaded across Angus' forehead as a lump rose in his throat. His hands slipped and grabbed again to get a better hold. His mind raced. What would he do once Ferock clamped its mouth shut and dove into the sea? He'd be swept down the sea monster's throat and drown for sure.

The sea monster belched, and more foul air rose from Ferock's putrid gut which caused Angus to almost lose his grip. He struggled to hold his breath to keep from inhaling the stench but it did little good. He gritted his teeth, and his muscles ached as he fought to hang on. One slip and Ferock would swallow him whole. Angus swung his legs until he could wedge his feet into a crook between Ferock's fangs. The monster shook his head, trying to shake Angus loose. But Angus only held on tighter, concentrating on not letting go. A cold chill surged in his veins. Dangling from one of the sea monster's teeth, Angus spotted a large lensed camera—the same one the man on the boat had been carrying.

Ferock's jaws unhinged, and the monster's tongue probed for him. The oozing appendage, slick as whale skin, smeared a layer of slime across Angus' neck and down to his wounded ankle. The tongue flicked over the injury, paused, and then was repelled.

A great grumble sounded deep within Ferock's gullet, and the beast arched its neck and retched, launching Angus out of its mouth and into the sea. Angus rocketed into the deep like a cannonball.

The painful plunge knocked the wind out of Angus. He struggled to the surface; his weary arms felt as if they were made of lead, and his lungs were on the verge of bursting. Exploding to the surface, wheezing for air, he swam with uncoordinated strokes toward shore, all the while expecting the sea monster at his heels. When he neared the island's edge, he shot a panicked glance over his shoulder, anticipating that Ferock would try to swallow him once again. To his surprise, he spotted the sea monster retreating at a steady pace in the opposite direction.

Vanora stretched out her hand, leaning over the water. "Over here!"

Angus made three more exhausted strokes, fighting an endless battle against the current that threatened to sweep him back out to sea. When he finally reached the rocky outcropping of the cave, Vanora grasped his hand and helped him onto the bank.

She knelt beside him. "Are you hurt, Angus?"

Angus shook his head and rolled onto his back, fighting to catch his breath and staring at the dark clouds floating overhead. "I'll live."

Vanora leaned over him and studied him for a moment. "That was really weird."

Angus sat up, still breathing hard. "Weird? Don't you mean terrifying?"

"No, it was weird. The way he just suddenly spit you out like a piece of bad meat and took off."

Angus frowned. "It was strange. It was like he didn't like the way my ankle tasted."

"Oh my gosh! Did he bite you?"

"No, thank goodness, but he ran his tongue over my wound and then puked me out."

Vanora smirked. "I'd gag too if I had someone's scummy foot in my mouth."

"Really?" Angus rolled onto his side. "I doubt you'd have enough room with your own stuffed in it half the time."

"Ha, ha, very funny." Vanora leaned closer, sniffed him, and pinched her nose. "Phew. You stink!"

"Thanks, it's a new kind of cologne. I put it on just for you—Eau de Barf for Smart Alecks."

Vanora flung Angus' shirt and shoes at him. "Hurry up and put these on. I'm worried sick about my dad."

Angus ducked. "Hey, take it easy would you?" He slipped on his shirt and tennis shoes and tried to stand. Pain radiated from his swollen ankle, and he yanked up his pant leg. The bite wound had now swelled to the size of an egg, and a long, vertical slit ran across it like a deep paper cut.

Vanora rolled her eyes. "What now?"

Angus grimaced. "My ankle's killing me."

"Let me have a look." Vanora crouched to examine the injury and cringed. "It's really swollen and—uh-oh."

"What's the matter?"

Vanora chewed her bottom lip and gave Angus a look that made his heart flip. "There's h-hairy things sticking out in the middle of it."

Angus sat on a large rock and eased his leg up over his knee to examine the wound. Two rows of bristly, black hair protruded from the injury. Angus ran his fingers along the stiff bristles. In a flash of pain, the gash split wide open. He jerked his hand back. "Ouch!"

Angus' throat constricted. He stared down at the aching wound, not wanting to believe what he was seeing.

An unblinking eye with a big black pupil glared back at him.

6

The Hall of Learning

"Cover it, quick!"

Angus stared down at the eye. "What is it?"

"I'm pretty sure it's a witch's eye! Prudence must have implanted it when she bit you. From what I've read about them, she can hear everything we do and see every road we travel." Vanora raised her eyebrows. "And worse yet, sometimes those eyes die and rot on the victim's leg, poisoning the person and…"

"Argh!" Angus twisted his leg to examine the thing. "It's disgusting! How do I get rid of it?"

The eye was almost solid black and void of expression. Angus reached a shaky hand out to touch it.

Vanora grabbed his arm. "Don't!"

He jerked away, but not before the tip of his index finger brushed against the pupil. The witch eye blinked furiously. Pain shot up his leg, all the way into his head. He slapped a hand over his eye. "Ouch! I felt that. So much for trying to poke it out… gross!"

"I tried to warn you. It's a part of you now. That's how the curse works."

"How do you get rid of it?"

"Beats me!" Vanora said. "Toss me the harp, and let's get going."

Angus dropped his pant leg, flinched as it brushed over the eye, and handed the harp to Vanora.

She cradled the instrument in her arms and rushed inside the cave. Her toe hit the end of a rock. Vanora lost her balance and pitched forward. The harp flew out of her hands.

"NO!" she screamed.

Angus leapt for it, landed on his belly, and caught it just before it went over the edge and into the bottomless water.

"Sorry, Angus!"

"It's okay. I got it." He handed the harp to Vanora. "Here, try to hold onto it this time." Angus got to his feet.

Vanora took the instrument, closed her eyes, and plucked the strings.

The walls shifted, grumbled, and split apart, revealing the ornate doors with raised panels engraved in silver. The MacBain crest stood etched in the center, surrounded by Celtic scrolls and knotwork. Angus reached inside his shirt, drew out the amulet, and inserted the tail of the dragon into the massive lock. The lock fell loose to one side, and he shoved hard on the old doors. The mammoth hasps groaned open, and they entered the Hall of Kings.

Angus groped along the wall until he found the hearth. Resting on the mantle, he uncovered a stack of wooden matches. He selected one and struck it against the stone wall until it sizzled into flame. Angus lit the tip of a nearby torch and surveyed the room.

Vanora put down the harp and grabbed a second torch from the wall. “Here, light mine.”

Angus touched his blazing torch to Vanora’s. It smoldered, and then finally a yellow glow formed at the tip. “According to the book,” Angus said, “the Hall of Learning should be next to the Hall of Kings.”

“Look!” Vanora waved her torch toward a narrow hallway behind the massive table. “It must be that way.” She took off before Angus could stop her.

“Wait!”

She stopped and rolled her eyes. “Come on! We don’t have all day. We have to save my father!”

“I know,” Angus said, lowering his voice. “Don’t you remember what Fane said about this place? Dark and vile things occupy it now.”

“No kidding, but there’s no other way. We have to go through the floor, which we know from last time only leads to all the halls *except* the Hall of Learning. Now come on.”

Vanora hurried down the narrow hallway. Angus followed cautiously. At the end of the short corridor, a doorway stood illuminated by a soft light. They hurried to the entrance surrounded by two immense, bronze statues. The one on the left was a life-size warrior clad in a kilt, holding a pike and leaning slightly backward, as if to gain momentum for throwing the weapon. In the palm of his right hand, two giant candles flickered. The other statue was a graceful, winged creature guarding marble books at its feet with a sword in its hand. On the tips of its wings were two iridescent lights.

Angus stepped around Vanora, grasped the big, iron door handle, and slowly pushed it open. Inside, more candles glowed. Hundreds of shelves lined each wall, and large, round tables sat in each corner. A cozy fire blazed in an open hearth. Something moved from behind a tall shelf.

Vanora grabbed his arm. "What's that?" she whispered.

A little old man stepped out of the shadows. He wore a long beard and a white robe that fell to his ankles. He pointed at Angus' chest.

"Is that a dragon amulet?"

Angus put his hand over it protectively. "Yes."

"Then you must be a descendent of the kings?"

Angus nodded. "I'm Angus—Angus MacBain, and this is my friend, Vanora."

The elderly man came close and lifted a candle wedge to Angus' face. The stranger's squinty eyes flashed, and he gasped. "It's been a long time, indeed, since a king has visited here." The man bowed and extended his hand. "Forgive me, Your Highness. Allow me to introduce myself. My name is Aed. I am a scribe and the caretaker of the ancient texts. You must excuse my poor manners; I wasn't expecting anyone, and it's been so many centuries since a mortal has visited the library. It's now used exclusively by wizards and other such beings."

Vanora frowned. "Centuries? You've been here that long?"

"Oh, yes. I've been a scribe here since the early times. And, of course, my work is never done." The man let out a long sigh. "If someone needs a text, I must transcribe it, as we don't allow the originals to be checked out. The enchanted quills do help of course, but they are always full of glitches, running out of ink and whatnot." He lowered his voice to a whisper. "And when they feel like they're overworked they can be temperamental and really write some terrible stuff—expletives mostly. Not for the faint of heart, if you know what I mean."

The old scribe stepped to one side, and Angus spotted movement on a desk near the fireplace. Ink pens scribbled madly across page after page of text. He nudged Vanora. "Wish I had something like that to do my homework."

The pens suddenly stopped in midair. Angus glanced at Vanora and frowned. "Something I said?"

The old man sighed. "They don't like to be watched. Sorry, but as I told you, they can be quite temperamental and extraordinarily rude at times. Best to just ignore them."

The pens went back to scribbling, and Angus strained to see what they were writing. *We have an important message for you, Sire,* they wrote. Angus crept closer.

"What is it?" Vanora whispered.

"I don't know. They say they have a message for me."

The pens clacked together as they scribbled out a crude picture. Angus moved in closer. His pulse quickened. The pens had drawn a picture of a staring pig wearing a crown with Angus' name scrawled across the top and the words: *it's not nice to stare.*

Vanora clamped a hand over her mouth, trying not to giggle. "Holy cow, Angus! Guess they don't like you watching over their shoulder." She threw her head back and burst out laughing.

Angus frowned. "Try to control yourself, will you?"

Vanora only laughed harder and then hugged Angus' arm. "I'm so sorry. It just feels good to laugh."

Angus cracked a smile. He couldn't really be mad at her, and he was happy to see her happy again. But the smile dropped quickly from her face as she examined the rows of books towering to the cathedral ceiling.

Aed gave Angus an inquisitive look. "What can I help you find, Your Highness?"

"We need information on how to break a curse—an invisibility curse—and we also need information on an object. Something taken from Iona. Something that allows people from other worlds to enter into ours, without aging."

The scribe narrowed his bushy brows. "Very difficult questions indeed. But first, let's start with the invisibility curse. We need to determine what kind it is."

Vanora whirled around, her voice cracking. "It was put on my father by a sea hag who works for Dragomir. We can feel he's there, but it's like he's frozen and can't speak."

"Oh dear, I'm afraid that one doesn't have a simple answer. If it were just a common crone who cast the spell, it would most likely wear off in time. Hopefully, this will be the case with your father as well."

"What if it doesn't wear off?"

The scribe shook his head. "That would be most unfortunate as he would wither away rapidly. We must wait and see what happens. If it doesn't wear off, we will have to work quickly to figure out another way to spare him."

"So there's nothing we can do now?" Angus asked.

"Time is the only answer. Sometimes guessing at solutions only makes the problem worse. You will have to wait it out and hope for the best." Aed gave Vanora a sympathetic look. "I'm sorry, dear, I wish I had a better answer for you."

Vanora glanced at the floor, and Angus put his hand on her shoulder. "I'm sure it's going to work out okay. Maybe by the time we get back, the spell will be broken. And we'll hurry and return as soon as we can, just in case it hasn't."

"Okay," Vanora said, barely speaking above a whisper.

Angus wished he could do more for her. He knew how much she loved her dad and how terrible it would be if anything happened to him.

"Now to your other question," Aed said. "I hope you are not talking about Fane Vargovic?"

"Yes, I'm afraid so," Angus said.

"Oh dear. I was hoping it wasn't him. He has been a great friend of mine for many years. It would be sad, indeed, to lose him." Aed looked to be deep in thought. "Let me think… Hmm—I've got it! The ancient book of world-hopping. The only question is, where can it be? Since we creatures don't enter your world so much anymore, it might just be in the stone vault, or perhaps somewhere here." The scribe raised the candle higher.

"Wow," Vanora said.

From floor to ceiling, the ancient texts, clay tablets, scrolls, and stone tables filled every space.

"Don't you have a catalog system?" Vanora asked.

"Oh, yes, of course. But it only works if you know the

exact title and language it was written in. It could take me some time, perhaps a year." The man whistled, and a large dragonfly buzzed to the end of his nose. "Blubberwart, show me the section of ancient texts written in English."

The insect zipped over the top of Angus' head and landed near a pile of books stacked neatly on one stone shelf. The old man's eyes lit up. "Very good! Not many are housed, which makes our job of searching through them much easier. Most are written in the language of trolls, elves, dragons and other non-mortals."

"Thank you, Blubberwart." The scribe stepped forward, gently removed a book sitting on top of the pile, blew off the dust, and handed it to Angus.

Angus took the book and ran his hand over the dusty cover. He opened the book, and it started to sing. A shadowy figure sitting in a dark corner that they hadn't noticed before swiveled around in a stone chair and told them to hush. It was a large man sitting next to a crone in a tall black hat and cape. The man was wrapped from head to toe in rags. But some of his features could still be made out. A mummy?

"Sorry about that," the scribe said. "I forgot, that's the audio edition. You must flip it over to the other side for words. And don't mind the mummy; he came all the way from Mesopotamia, and he's quite crabby because he's suffering from an incurable itch..."

Angus scratched at his neck and flipped the volume over. He ran a finger down the table of contents and stopped at 'Objects Needed for Transportation.' He turned to page nineteen-hundred-and-sixty-nine. "It says two objects must be in place for transportation to and from Iona. One at the place of departure and one on the island of Iona." Angus glanced at Vanora. "Twin objects. If an item is taken from either location, the traveler can become trapped between worlds."

"Does it say what the objects are?" Vanora asked. "Anything to give us a clue?"

Angus shook his head. "It says, 'In order to find the particular objects for each place of travel, you must play the king's table, for it will tell you all you need to know.'"

Vanora looked at Aed. "What's the king's table? Is it some kind of game?"

"No, it's not really a game. More like a puzzle. It's a table built long ago to store information for the kings. They feared that if they wrote certain things down, it would be too easy for others to find out their secrets."

"Where is it?" Angus asked.

"It's in the Hall of Kings, of course. But you better hurry; you don't want to be in there after dark. I'll spare you the details, but there are a lot of dangerous beasts that lurk there."

"Come on!" Angus grabbed Vanora's hand. "Let's go."

He suddenly fell to his knees, grabbing his ankle. Vanora knelt beside him.

"What is it? What's wrong, Angus?"

"My ankle. It feels like it's on fire."

Angus pulled up his pant leg.

Aed shook his head. "Oh, this isn't good. Not good at all." The scribe shook his head slowly. "I'm very sorry, young King, but you're not going anywhere. Not until we take care of that ankle. Tell me how it happened, and don't leave out a single detail."

"I was bitten by a sea hag. The next thing I knew, my ankle started to hurt, and then this gross eye-thing formed."

Aed paled. "If we don't get rid of that eye, the sea hag who hexed you will see, hear, and know all that you do. More importantly, if we don't get rid of that eye, it will start to rot after a few days and eat through your ankle until you lose your foot or your leg."

"Wow," Vanora said. "How horrible, and the smell would be—"

"Oh my gosh!" Angus snapped. "Seriously? Knock it off already!"

"Sorry about that," Vanora said, sheepishly. Her eyes widened. "But you know, I've heard that—"

Angus glared at her. "Do you ever stop?"

"Guess not…" Vanora slapped a hand over her mouth.

Angus groaned and turned to Aed. "How can we get rid of this thing?"

"Come with me." They followed Aed through a dimly lit passageway that led to a chamber at the back of the library. They came to a heavy, wooden door with long, metal hinges and a gargoyle for a knocker in the center. Aed opened a heavy door that led into living quarters. A fire blazed in the corner, a simple cot stood along one wall with a plain brown blanket, and a deep, leather chair sat in front of the fire with a round footstool. A kettle boiled above the flames.

"You better wait here, Miss." Aed motioned Vanora to the chair by the fire. "No matter what you may hear, it's best that you don't interfere. If the healing process is interrupted, it can make the curse even stronger and harder to break."

Angus wrung his hands. "Okay, let's get this over with."

Vanora plopped down into the chair, giving Angus a worried look. "What, exactly, are you going to do to him?"

"Just a simple poultice, but it can burn like the dickens." Aed hurried into a small kitchen and returned carrying several skinny jars filled with an assortment of herbs and strange-looking twigs and roots. He mixed them in a marble bowl with a large masher. The mixture steamed and burned Angus' eyes.

Aed studied Angus' head. "I need one more thing from you before the mixture is complete—a lock of your hair. Would that be okay with you?"

Angus nodded. "Just try not to leave me a bald spot."

Aed picked up a pair of scissors, cut a dark brown curl from Angus' temple, and dropped it into the mixture. A puff of smoke rose from the concoction. Once mixed, the scribe led Angus into another room, this one void of all furnishings except for two arm shackles attached to the stone wall.

"Wait a second," Angus said. "Why would a scribe have shackles?"

"In the olden times, they were used to keep dark and evil creatures captive for the MacBain kings. In more recent times, it's for those who can't keep quiet in the library."

Angus' eyes went wide. "Really? Wow."

Aed chuckled and shook his head. "Just a joke, young king—about the library, I mean. But I'm serious about the kings. They were insistent about law and order. When they were busy traveling between here and Ceòban, they didn't like problems. Sadly, since the kings have all been gone, the vile things that live in the dark have multiplied." Aed cleared his throat. "I want to commend you for your bravery and loyalty to Fane Vargovic. It is a most admirable virtue."

"Thank you," Angus said. He didn't feel he deserved to be commended. There was a part of him that just wanted to go home, to not have to fight dark creatures, to take the easy way out—but deep inside he wanted to help Fane more than anything. He'd come to love the old man like a father.

"If you agree, Sire, I think it's best to have your arms bound so that you can't touch your eyes. For if you do the curse will not be broken. Any weakness, and it will thrive. You must do your best to beat it. But it's a nasty business."

"No, I don't want to be shackled. No offense, but I'm not that trusting."

"None taken, but I must insist again that you do not touch your eyes, even though they will burn like fire. Do you understand?"

Angus nodded. Aed brought him a stool, and Angus sat as the scribe applied the paste to his ankle. Nothing happened. Angus frowned. "I don't feel anything."

"That's because I'm not done yet. We must cover it. That is when the pain will start." The scribe paused and then frowned. "I'm very sorry about this. It will probably be something you will remember the rest of your life. Try to be as brave as you can." Aed grabbed a patch of burlap with a shaky hand, took a deep breath, and said, "Are you ready, Sire?"

Angus studied Aed's face. The wrinkles in the scribe's face deepened.

Angus nodded.

"Best to shut your eyes now, Your Highness."

Angus gritted his teeth and closed his eyes.

Aed placed the patch on Angus' ankle. A pain so deep and severe shot into his head that Angus had to bite into his lip to keep from screaming. He grabbed the sides of the stool. An intense heat filled his eyes. At first, it felt as if he had gotten soap into them; then, slowly, even though he thought it couldn't get any worse, the pain intensified. Angus struggled to open his eyes, but when he did he couldn't see. He fell to his knees as a scream clawed its way out of his throat. He squeezed his eyes shut. Behind his searing eyelids, demons and horrible winged beasts shrieked and flapped in rage.

After what seemed like an eternity, each terrible beast faded. With them, so did the pain in his eyes and ankle.

Aed's hand rested on Angus' shoulder. "It won't be much longer, now. Hold tight."

Angus waited. And waited.

Finally, Aed ripped the patch from his flesh. By now, the pain was a mere ache. Through blurry eyes that hurt with every flicker of light, Angus examined his ankle. The eye looked to be bleeding and oozing, melting into gelatinous goo sliding across his skin.

"That's good," Aed said. "It's melting. It should be nothing but a small, red spot, soon." He grabbed a jar from the fireplace mantel. Opening the lid, he stuck his fingers inside and pulled out a layer of thick goop. Aed applied the glutinous blob to Angus' ankle.

"That should take the sting out of it."

Angus took a deep breath. He felt like he'd just run a mile-long race. "Thank you."

Aed nodded. "We need to patch your ankle with herbs to prevent infection and to keep the eye from growing back. There's a high recurrence rate if we don't." The scribe scratched his beard. "I believe a few bits of Chinese parsley, Elf Leaf, and Umakhuthula should do the trick."

Aed reached for a flask, poured water onto a bit of cloth, and stuck his fingers into various jars. Taking a pinch of this and a dab of that, he placed it all into a round bowl. Using a large stone as a pestle, he crushed several herbs together and added it to the compress. He handed Angus the cool material. "Hold this against your eyes. It will help."

Angus pressed it to his face. The soothing cloth eased the burn in his eyes.

"It should heal quickly, now." Aed helped Angus out of the room and to a cot near the fire.

Vanora rushed to Angus' side. "Are you okay?"

Angus nodded and settled into the thin, scratchy mattress, every bit of his energy spent.

"He will need to rest now," Aed said. "Eye exorcism is nasty business. It's very hard on the body and soul."

"I don't have time to rest." Angus stood but suddenly the floor seemed to move beneath his feet. He lost his balance and toppled over. Aed caught him before he crashed to the floor. "Put your arm around my neck, and let's get you to the cot."

Angus sat gently on the small bed.

Vanora knelt at his side. “You have to rest, Angus. I need your help. I can’t do this alone. You have to get your strength back if we’re going to save Fane and my dad.”

“I know; I’m sorry. I just feel like I should be doing more.” Angus laid down, and Vanora covered him with a woolen blanket.

She pulled a chair beside the cot and lowered her head into her hands.

Aed rested a hand on her shoulder. “I understand you must be concerned, child.” The scribe sighed. “It’s a terrible worry for one so young. He’ll need a short rest until the last bits of the curse have gone—then it’s off you go.”

Angus fought to stay awake. Thoughts of Fane and Mr. Pegenstecher played over and over in his mind until sleep pulled his aching eyes closed.

7

The King's Table

Angus awoke with a start, his throat dry and his head aching. Vanora stood waiting by his bedside. He shielded his eyes from the blinding light, which hurt more and more with every blink. "How long was I out?"

"I don't know," Vanora said. "It seemed like forever. I'd guess at least two hours."

Angus sat up, his head spinning. He tossed the covers to the side and got to his feet, gripping the mantelpiece to keep from tipping over. "We have to get going. I can't believe we lost so much time." Angus rubbed his eyes, and a sharp pain seared into his eyelids. He focused on Vanora's blurry face. "Why didn't you wake me sooner?"

"I tried—but I couldn't get you to snap out of it! You just kept snoring away."

"Snoring? I don't snore."

"Uh... yeah, you do. And I hate to break it to you, Angus, but you snore really loud. In fact, it's so loud it reminds me of a big, old—"

"Okay, I get it!" Angus snapped. "You don't have to go into detail."

"I just thought you might want to know. Maybe you should buy some of those nose strips. You know, they sell them online, and you can just order them and have them delivered to Iona."

"Look, I couldn't care less about nose strips or snoring or whatever right now."

"You know, I'm just as worried as you are. You don't have to be so crabby."

"Sorry, it's just my eyes are all blurry and they hurt like…"

Aed entered the room and came to Angus' side. "Here." He extended his hand.

Angus stared down into the scribe's palm. Two clear worms, each about four inches long, squiggled, then jumped up and down like tiny corkscrews.

Vanora wrinkled her nose. "Eww, what are those things?"

"Eye gummies. To get the full benefit, you must use them right away."

Angus peered at the squiggly things and frowned. "Use them how? Hope you aren't meaning I have to eat them…"

Aed shook his head and chuckled. "No, no, of course not. You put them in your eyes. They conform to the shape of your eyeballs. Most people are opposed to putting worms into their eyes, but these are a special breed. They are very soothing. Used for healing purposes. I think you will find them most useful."

Angus held out his hand and grimaced. Aed was right; he didn't like the idea of worms in his eyes. The fat, little grubs sprang up and down in his palm, cold as ice. Angus jumped and nearly dropped them.

Aed lifted Angus' hand. "Hold them steady and draw them up near your eyes. They will settle right in and give you a lot of comfort. Think of them as friends."

Angus shuddered. Some friends they were. He hated the way they squirmed in his palm. He slowly moved his hand up to his face. Without warning, the worms sprang into the corner of each of his eyes and then flattened out. Angus' first instinct was to rub his eyes and get the worms out, but they felt so soothing, so cool. The worms were transparent, and although his vision was still blurry, he was able to see. Within moments, the throbbing pain had eased, and his vision had cleared.

"Wow, that does feel a lot better," Angus said.

"Yes, they are very effective. But just don't forget to take them out," Aed said. "If they get bored they can be very mischievous."

Vanora cocked her head and smiled. "How so?"

Angus groaned. "You would have to ask."

Vanora scrunched up her face. "Well, it's better to know, isn't it? Rather than be surprised?" Vanora lowered her voice. "I'm really disappointed in you sometimes, Angus. You have absolutely no curiosity about the things around you. You would much rather hide your head in the sand than figure things out by asking a few simple questions."

"That's not true!" Angus protested.

Vanora raised an eyebrow.

"Okay, maybe you're right." Angus sighed as he turned

to the scribe. "What do they do?"

Aed shrugged. "Nothing in particular. They're just little devils. They can drive people insane by making them think they're seeing things. But that's only when they've become bored and want out. Can't say I blame them. Wouldn't be much of a life, living in someone's eyeballs. Plus, they like the dark and damp as they are cold-blooded beings. This cave is perfect for them. And they have families to get back to, of course."

"Families?" Vanora asked.

"Never mind that," Angus groaned. "How do I get them out when I'm done with them?"

"That's very simple. Hold out your hand, and ask them to leave. They will jump right into your palm. Just don't drop them—they are quite fragile. Gently set them on the floor, and they will find their own way back."

"All right," Angus said. "Thanks."

They turned to leave when Aed spoke up. "Just a moment, there is one more thing. You'll need light. As you know, the passageway is as dark and grim as a grave." He handed each of them a burning torch and led them out of the Hall of Learning. "Do be careful. Come back if you need anything at all."

"We will, thank you," Vanora said.

Angus shook the man's hand and headed into the dark.

As they rushed through the passageway, their torchlight flickered along the stone walls.

They rounded a corner into The Hall of Kings. The room was just as Angus remembered. It was a large cave, maybe forty paces from wall to wall. High above his head, jagged stalactites glistened. A fireplace with an iron caldron and a rocky mantel stood in ruin, caked with a film of fine dust and silt. An enormous table of cut stone rested in the center of the room.

Angus held his torch high, walking briskly to the big, round table, with Vanora close behind. She brushed her hand across the stone surface, swiping away dirt and grime. Leaning in close to the table, she squinted at it. "I don't see any special markings or anything."

Angus ran his fingers underneath one side of the table. "Wait a second; I feel something on the bottom. Maybe we need to flip it over."

"How? This thing must weight a ton—at least."

"I don't know." Angus stared at the massive table. "There has to be a way."

"We've just started, and already I feel exhausted." Vanora went to sit in one of the tall stone chairs.

"Don't!" Angus shouted.

Vanora jumped to her feet. "Why? What is it?"

"Don't you remember how the chairs lowered through the floor when we were here before? I'd stay clear of them if I were you. You might be taken on a ride to a place you don't want to go."

"Sorry, guess I'm not thinking straight. I just keep worrying about my dad." Vanora's voice cracked. "It's just so hard."

"I'm worried too, but worrying about it won't do us any good. In fact, it only makes things worse. As hard as it is, you need to believe that everything is going to be okay. Just try not to think about it. He'll be okay." Angus squeezed Vanora's hand. "I promise."

"I know you're right. It's just so hard." Vanora turned

her attention to the table. "There has to be a seam somewhere." She put her torch into a holder on the wall. "The table has to come apart somehow."

"Here." Angus handed Vanora his torch. "Hang mine up too, please." Vanora stuck the torch into the wall while Angus ran his hand over the table's stone surface. A ridge running down the center rippled beneath his fingers. "You're right! I can feel it. Pull on your side and I'll pull on this side."

They gave it a firm tug, but the tabletop didn't move.

"Wait!" Vanora ducked her head underneath the table. There's a latch under here." She pulled something, and a ping echoed through the dark chamber. "See if you have one on your side, Angus."

Angus groped the underside until his hand bumped a metal bar. He pulled it aside, and something clicked.

"Okay," Vanora said. "Let's try again."

With one giant tug, the table groaned as the sections slid apart, the sides folded, and the top flipped upside down and snapped together again.

"Wow, it's amazing!" Vanora exclaimed.

"Look!" Angus pointed to the side of the table. "There's a bag!"

Angus eased the bag free. He opened the drawstring and dumped a bunch of carved stone figurines onto the table. Each was a different shape and color. There was a sword, a ship's wheel, a dog, an oak tree, and a white horse. The last figure was an island.

"What are we supposed to do with them?" Angus asked.

"I think you have to pick the one that will tell you the answer you're looking for."

Angus shuffled through the figurines. Nothing seemed to match what he was looking for. Then he picked up the small one shaped like an island. Its edges were made of gold. "I think this is Iona." Angus flipped it over and squinted. "It says *Ì Chaluim Chille.*"

"That's Gaelic for Iona!" Vanora exclaimed. "Maybe it will tell us what we need to know!"

Angus frowned at the table. "What do we do with it?"

Vanora wiped off the rest of the surface. "There has to be a place to insert it… like a token."

Angus grabbed a torch from the wall and held it high, following Vanora as she cleared away the dust.

"Here!" She coughed. "There's a hole in the center of the table."

Angus handed Vanora the torch, leaned forward, and dropped the carved stone into the hole where it clanked down inside and disappeared. They waited. Nothing happened. Vanora frowned. "Maybe there's a lever you have to push?"

Angus felt all along the table. "No. But the top is wobbly… I wonder if it spins?"

Vanora shrugged. "Give it a try."

Angus gripped the sides of the massive table and heaved it to one side. The table whipped round and round, spinning faster and faster, and then suddenly it came to a grinding stop. The floor rumbled and then shook. A slot in the middle of the table opened, and out rolled a series of stones. Together they spelled out a single word—Tavish.

"What's a Tavish?"

"It's a Gaelic word. It means twin," Vanora whispered.

Angus sighed. "We already knew we were looking for

two of the same objects."

"Yes, but it must mean something important."

"Like what?"

Vanora shrugged. "I think we need to go back to the library and do some more research."

Angus groaned. "I just hope we find some answers quick. We're running out of time."

They started to leave the room when Angus remembered he was still holding the bag of figures.

"Wait." Angus hung the bag back on the side of the table. The table groaned, spun around, and put itself back together again.

They hurried to the library where Aed was busy putting books away with Blubberwart buzzing nearby. The scribe turned to face them, giving them a quizzical look. "Back already?"

"'Fraid so. The table didn't tell us much—just that we're looking for twin objects. But we already knew that."

Aed frowned. "That's very strange, indeed. That's all it said? Are you sure?"

"Yeah. It said 'Tavish'."

Aed's eyes sprang wide. "I should have known! King MacBain's wildcat, Tavish! Such a likeable feline, but savage and fearless in battle. He was no normal housecat. Massive across the chest—bigger than any lion. He was born in Ceòban and given as a gift to the kindly king for protection."

Vanora sucked in a breath. "I saw a cat—a huge one, carved of white stone, resting on top of one of the ancient tombstones in the cemetery! That has to be the one. It's very old and weathered, but I knew it was a cat by the deeply carved whiskers." She glanced at Angus. "It could easily be broken and taken from the island."

Angus looked at the floor. "It could be anywhere by now. Especially if Cudweed took it; he probably tossed it into the sea."

"Cudweed?" Aed asked.

"He's an evil crow who works for Dragomir," Angus said. "He can turn into a creepy old man at will. He also works for a sea hag who pretended to be my aunt. She's the one who cursed me with that eye."

Vanora nodded. "He escaped a couple months ago. But somehow they're back again—at least the sea hag is. We thought we had turned her into sludge, but I guess not."

"I imagine when the crow snatched the cat, he knew it would weaken the protective force field between the worlds, and the sea hag would be able to make her reappearance. You see, even from the grave, Dragomir's psychic powers prevail. It's like trying to bury oil. The slippery substance seeps to the surface from time to time."

"So where do we start looking for the object?" Angus asked.

Aed shook his head sadly. "I wish I knew."

"Can we use a substitute? A different object?" Vanora asked.

Aed shook his head. "It must be from the age of the kings and blessed with a certain spell. Your best bet is to find its twin. I know they forged a third one in the event one was lost, misplaced, or stolen, as in this case." Aed shook his head again and frowned. "I wish I knew where to tell you to begin. But only the kings and perhaps a handful of others would have known."

Vanora scanned the vast reaches of the library. "Are there any books that would tell us?"

Aed shook his head. "I'm afraid not. It wouldn't be something they'd want recorded. It could have gotten into the wrong hands. They had to be very careful." Aed stroked his long, white beard. "We might catch a glimpse of it in The Book of Pictures." The scribe turned. "Blubberwart, get me the ancient book of textiles."

Blubberwart buzzed off, flying to a top shelf near the ceiling. He gripped a large volume with his thin feet, tugged it free, and flew back to the table, struggling with the heavy book. Aed grabbed it before it fell. He laid the book on the table and carefully opened its golden pages.

"This beautiful volume was made by a great artist who worked for the kings during the time King MacBain traveled frequently between here and Ceòban. King MacBain and his men were collecting weapons for war among the humans. At that time, a lot of history was recorded in pictures as well as in written word." Aed pushed the book to Angus. "Grab only the top corner to turn the pages."

Angus studied the book. The print looked so blurry. Every time he tried to focus, it only made things worse. "Wait a second." Angus held out his hands. "Okay, you can get out now."

Into his palms jumped the eye gummies. He set them on the table. He rubbed his eyes and then watched the worms squiggle away.

Angus scanned every page, hoping to find something fast. He sighed when he got to the end. "I didn't see anything."

"You were going too fast," Vanora said. "Let me take a look. You have to study each page. You can't just whiz past."

"All right, take a look." Angus maneuvered the large book so that it sat in front of her. Vanora stared at the beginning page so long that Angus grew anxious. Finally, she began to flip though the book, studying each section. When she neared the end, Angus' heart sank. But then Vanora flipped the page. "There!" she said.

She slid the book back in front of Angus and tapped on a picture. It was a depiction of a perfectly square, stone room with several slabs for shelves. On each shelf was an object, and on the very top shelf sat a cat made of white stone, wedged in between two gargoyles.

Vanora shouted with glee. "It's the same one I saw in the cemetery!"

Several ghostly figures in the library turned in their seats and hushed her.

"You're right!" Angus said.

"Please be quiet!" A ghostly figure wearing a kilt and broadsword floated near.

"Sorry," Angus said.

The ghost left in a huff.

Angus leaned close to Vanora and whispered. "Guess we should be quiet before we get tossed out of here."

"Sorry."

The ghostly figures turned back around and continued reading their newspapers.

"It's a storage room!" Vanora whispered. She turned to Aed. "Do you recognize where it's at?"

Aed looked pale. "Yes, I'm afraid I do. It's not a good place. Not good at all."

"What do you mean?" Angus asked.

Aed's shoulders dropped. He pointed to a spot in the book. "You see that mark along the wall, just outside of the vault?"

Angus and Vanora nodded.

"It means danger or beware. They put the vault someplace where no mortal would dare to tread without a king's army for protection."

"So where is it?" Angus asked.

"It's in the Hall of Dargis."

Vanora paled. "You mean…" She shuddered. "… where those rat-things live?"

Aed nodded slowly.

Angus put a hand on Vanora's shoulder. "It's okay, Vanora. You can stay here, and I'll go and get it. You don't have to do this. I know how you feel about rats… especially those kinds of rats."

Vanora frowned. "You know I won't let you go alone. My father's life is at stake. We're in this together, remember?"

"I know, but I want you to know it's okay," Angus said. "I can do it alone if you don't want to come with me."

"No! I'm going, and that's final."

"The doorway is hidden," Aed said. "That is where your agate eyeglass will come in handy."

Angus' eyes widened. "How did you know about my eyeglass?"

"Everyone knows the king has one. Every MacBain king has had it. It's been handed down through the centuries. The eyeglass shows pictures of the past, and it makes a handy magnifier. But more importantly, it's a weapon to use against the ghosts and ghouls and other dark beings."

"An eyeglass?" Vanora said. "How can an eyeglass be a weapon?"

Aed's voice dropped into low, whispered tones. "When there is an evil presence, the eyeglass shines a very bright light. This is a powerful tool in the war against those who work for Lord Dragomir—especially his wraiths. They are frightening and terrible entities. They arise from the shadows or out of cracks and crevices in the stone walls when least expected. They can pass right through you and drain the warmth from your body." Aed paused and looked hard at Angus. "These vile beasts were men once. Great kings, knights, and warriors, who chose to be consumed with evil in life. In death, Dragomir rewarded them for their ghastly deeds by allowing them to live on, serving him and doing his dark bidding. You must take great care to avoid them at all costs. You won't find them in the Hall of Dargis though. They avoid it for some reason. Take great care not to get turned out or lost; it's a smelly, vile place, and there are many pathways."

"Thanks for the advice. Last time we entered the Hall of Dargis with Fane, he gave us some chalk so we could make a doorway to get out if we needed to. Do you have any?" Angus asked.

"Oh, yes, of course, and I have something else, as well."

With a swish of his robes, the scribe hurried into the back room and returned with two sticks of chalk and a large, purple sack. "Tuck the chalk into your pockets, and keep this bag safe. Inside are a dozen dodo eggs. They're the only things that can appease the rats. So, if you get into trouble, toss them at their feet. Like all rodents, they love raw eggs."

Vanora raised her eyebrows. "Wait a second. Dodos have been extinct for hundreds of years. How could you possibly have their eggs?"

"Yes," chuckled Aed. "Of course they have—but only in your world, my dear."

Angus reached into the bag and cradled one of the oval eggs. He ran his fingers over the smooth, white shell, which was speckled with reddish-brown spots.

Aed held up a cautious hand. "Take care that you don't break one here; they smell worse than woolly rhino dung. We'd all have to be evacuated."

Angus carefully placed the egg back in the sack and handed it to Vanora. "Is there a shortcut to the Hall of Dargis?"

"I'm afraid not," Aed said. "But I can show you a very helpful atlas. You won't be able to take it with you, of course, but it will be most helpful to show you the way."

"That would be great," Angus said. "We've been to the Hall of Dargis before, but we came a different way."

Aed nodded, "Yes, of course. Where did I put that book?" He scratched his head as if deep in thought and then a wide grin spread across his face. "I remember! Come this way, please." He hurried to his desk at the head of the library and reached beneath it. He pulled out a large, leather-bound volume. "Here we are! *The Atlas of Strange and Unusual Places in Fingal's Cave*."

He flipped open the book to the middle and tapped a

couple places on the page. "There are several ways you can get there, but this is the quickest from here."

Angus studied the illustration. "So, we go through the Hall of Kings again."

"And then pretty much follow the main tunnel," Vanora added.

The grin fell from the scribe's face. He knitted his brows and then opened his mouth as if to say something, but instead, he gave Angus a low bow. "Good luck to you, Your Highness, and safe journey."

Angus shook the man's hand. "Thanks again for everything," Angus said. "You've helped us a lot, and we won't forget it."

Vanora and Angus started to walk away when the scribe spoke up again.

"Do take care," Aed said.

"We will. Thanks again." Angus turned to Vanora. "I've been thinking. Maybe you should stay here where it's safe."

Vanora narrowed her eyes and planted her hands on her hips. "You can't be serious, can you?"

"I know you're worried about your dad, but…"

"I'm going, and that's final," Vanora snapped. "I have to make sure we get the statue and get back to my dad. Plus, I want to keep an eye on you. You don't always make the best decisions, Angus."

"What are you talking about? It's you that seems to get us into trouble. You're always so curious about stuff and…"

"So I should just go along with everything you dream up? Not check things out first, but just dive right on in?

Is *that* what you're saying?"

"What I'm trying to say is that you never listen. You always dream up some horrible scenario that I can't get out of my head."

"So that's all I do? Fill your head with terrible things? Maybe I should remind you of all the help I've given you, and—"

"Never mind all that. We don't have time to argue about it now. Forget it, and let's move on."

"You started it, Angus." Vanora sighed.

"I know; I'm sorry I said anything at all. To be honest, I'm glad you're going with me. It's better to have company than to go alone, anyhow. Plus, you do help when you're not gabbing so much."

"Gabbing?"

"Come on!" Angus groaned. "Let's go before we lose any more precious time."

Angus and Vanora hurried to The Hall of Kings. Thankfully, Vanora remained quiet. Angus didn't like squabbling with her. It just seemed to make him all the more weary. They entered the hall and rushed to the stone table.

"Do you remember which seat is yours?" Angus asked.

Vanora bit her lower lip. "I think so. It was either that one—" Vanora pointed to a big chair across from Angus. "—or the one beside it."

"Be absolutely sure. You know what happens if you sit in the wrong one... it will buck you off."

"How could I forget?"

They each sat in their seat and waited.

Vanora frowned. "Nothing's happening."

"Maybe we need to give it a few more minutes."

After more time passed, Angus leaned forward. "Are you sitting all the way back in your seat?"

"No, not really."

"Why not?"

"Because I'm not totally sure if this is the right one or not."

"I don't mean to sound like a jerk, but we don't have all day. Just do it, and hope for the best."

"That's easy for you to say. You get King MacBain's chair. His is easy to tell. Mine looks just like all the others." Vanora pointed to the other chairs surrounding Angus'. She was right; they all did look alike, except for the scrollwork that lined the top of each one.

"I wish I could do it for you, but I can't. Try to not think about, er, well… broken bones and stuff."

"Oh, that helps," Vanora huffed. "Thanks a lot. Now who's being all gory?"

"I'm sorry, but you know what I mean. We've got to hurry, and you're taking forever."

"Just give me a second, okay?" Vanora inhaled a deep breath and scrunched her eyes closed. She cautiously settled back into the chair.

The stone floor rumbled. Angus grabbed the armrests of his chair. His seat lurched forward, then back. It shook again before it finally started to lower through a crack in the floor. Dust, thick and heavy, clouded Angus' view of Vanora as the Hall of Kings disappeared above them. They sank downward until the chairs stopped with a thud in a dark chamber dimly lit with torches on the wall.

Angus stood, grabbed a torch, and held it in front of him. Nearby, Vanora coughed dust from her lungs.

"Are you okay?"

"Yeah, but this place is filthy! It could sure use a good dusting."

Angus walked ahead, burning away thick drapes of cobwebs with the flame.

"Ugh, that stinks." Vanora stayed close behind him.

"Don't touch the webbing," Angus warned. "Remember what Fane said—it's as sharp as knives and will cut to the bone." Angus continued to burn the dangerous webbing away from the walls. Something scurried past, and Vanora screamed.

"It's okay," Angus said. "I think it's gone now. Uh-oh…"

"What?"

Angus looked down at his shirt-pocket. A very bright light emanated from the thin material of his T-shirt. "The eyeglass is glowing."

Vanora gasped. "That means something evil is nearby, right? Isn't that what Aed said?"

Angus nodded and took a cautious step forward. Several black spiders scurried into their path. They were large and furry.

Vanora shrieked. She grabbed the back of Angus' T-shirt. "What are we going to do?"

"Back away slowly, and I'll deal with them. I'm sure they are the same spiders we took care of before. They hate fire, remember?"

"But there are so many of them. We only had one to deal with before."

"Just stay behind me. I'll take care of them."

Vanora took one step backward, and the spiders scurried toward them. They had eight jointed legs and two short forelegs that ended with giant, clacking pincers.

They rushed forward, snapping at Angus' head. He leapt back, waving the torch at the beasts. The biggest of the spiders lunged, knocking Angus to the ground. Vanora rushed from behind, kicking the giant arachnid. It snapped at her leg, crawling over Angus to get at her. Angus grabbed hold of the spider's legs. He slammed it against the wall over and over with all his might. It slid to the floor, twitched a few times, and leaked a pool of putrid, green liquid from its hairy thorax. Its shovel-like jaws clacked open, spitting and spewing dagger-like webbing everywhere. The spider twisted again. Its jaws closed, and it fell silent.

"I think it's dead, but just in case, be careful." Angus held his torch high and watched as the other insects backed away and disappeared into fissures in the walls.

"That thing was huge! I guess the others know better than to mess with us."

"Don't be so sure," Angus said. "They still might be up to something."

Vanora spun around. "Look." She pointed to several pairs of glowing eyes. They're staring at us—watching our every move." She paused. "I wonder why they aren't attacking?"

Angus shook his head. "Hard to say; maybe they don't want to die like their leader."

They groped their way through the dark corridor and down a set of stone steps.

"Isn't this where that ghost—Deadwood, or whatever his name is—lives?"

"IT'S WOODWORM, YOU NINNY!"

Vanora shrieked, and Angus nearly tripped down the last step as Woodworm swished past them.

"I thought I got rid of you last time!" Woodworm floated closer. "How can I rest with all this blasted commotion?"

"Look, we're not here to bother you. We just need to find the Hall of Dargis to get something we need."

"The Hall of Dargis? Why on earth would you want to go in there?"

"Just… nevermind. If you aren't going to help, then leave us alone." Angus gritted his teeth. "And don't come creeping up behind us wailing or something. It's the last thing we need right now."

"Well, all right, suit yourself then. I'll go back to napping. Don't say I didn't warn you. If something happens, please don't haunt this place." Woodworm shot them an annoyed look. "I'd hate to put up with you two for all eternity."

Woodworm floated away, and Angus paused to make sure the apparition was really gone. A round passageway loomed in front of them. Angus knew immediately that it was the right one as it was filled with jagged stalactites hanging from the ceiling. Scummy water dripped down their pointed blades, forming deep and murky ponds.

"I'd watch out for the thing that lives in those pools!" Woodworm said.

Angus jumped. "I thought you were gone!"

"Sorry, just couldn't pull myself away. It's like waiting

for a bloody accident to happen."

Vanora let out a terrified cry. "Something's got me!"

Angus whirled his torch around and saw a creature rising from one of the pools, its clawed hand gripping the back of Vanora's shirt. The monster had reptile-like skin and a long snout. It stood on two legs and had limbs like a crocodile. Angus slashed at the beast with his torch. The creature let loose of Vanora's shirt, dropped back into the pool, and disappeared.

"What was that?"

Angus shook his head. "I don't know, but it was really freaky."

"Terrible beasts!" Woodworm said. "They are made from the souls of men who have drowned in the sea. Men who knew only evil their whole lives." Woodworm yawned. "They aren't really dangerous… unless they're hungry."

Angus turned to Vanora. "Are you okay?"

She nodded. "Yeah, but I hate this creepy place!"

"Stay close and you'll be okay. Don't get near any more pools."

"No problem!" Vanora huffed. "The water is so gross."

"Follow me." Angus held his torch high. They carefully weaved between the shallow ponds and along the narrow path, pressing forward.

A putrid scent of decay seeped from the gloomy walls. Slimy sea snakes undulated in the next few pools. They loomed just under the surface, as if waiting for someone to take a wrong step so they could slither around unsuspecting feet and suck their prey under.

Angus raised his torch over the stagnant waters. The

flickering light revealed another huge beast gliding across the surface. The thing arched a crusty spine, leapt toward the light, and plunged back into the inky depths. Angus shivered and pressed forward.

A few moments later, they came to a massive stone door, braced on each side by two megalithic stones, their surfaces deeply etched with interlacing circles and the symbol of a seal. In the center, under a layer of dust, were letters shaped like thin willow sticks. Angus recognized them immediately. It was in his mother's tongue, the language of the Selkies.

"We're finally here. The Hall of Dargis."

"Good job!" Woodworm exclaimed. "Now this is where we say goodbye. For real this time."

"Goodbye." Angus glared at the ghost. Even though he annoyed Angus, there was a part of him that wanted Woodworm to stick around, to help guide them.

"Hope you make it out alive! Farewell!" Woodworm disappeared in an orange mist.

8

The Hall of Dargis

Angus lifted the chains carefully from the door, remembering how he had stupidly let them clatter to the floor before, alerting the horrible rodents inside.

Angus glanced at Vanora. "Are you ready?"

She pulled an egg from the sack. "Yup."

Angus shoved hard on the massive doors. He winced as they creaked open, louder than he had hoped. Vanora took a step inside.

Angus reached for her shoulder. "You better let me go first. Just in case."

"Ugh, I'd forgotten how much it stinks!" Vanora waved her free hand in front of her nose. "Stinking rats' nest."

"I know. I can hardly keep from gagging." Angus moved around her to take the lead. He held the torch in front of him, his eyes burning from the stench of the place.

They made their way down the long, dark corridor

stretching out in front of them. The floor was littered with what looked like moldy straw, scattered bones, crustaceans, and beastly carcasses Angus didn't want to identify. The end of the corridor rounded into two choices—a left or right tunnel. A dragging, scuttling sound made them stop.

"What was that?" Vanora whispered.

"Shh." Angus strained to see in the murky darkness. Just then, out of the corner of his eye, the tip of a long tail slithered around the left corner. A bloodcurdling shriek caused him to jump. He dropped his torch into a pool of foul water. The flame sizzled and winked out. They were cast into total darkness. Angus wheeled around, his heart pounding.

A scream sounded behind him. Vanora! Where was she? Angus froze, his own raspy breath his only companion. A light flashed before him, then blazed. Woodworm floated in front of him, torch in hand, searching the room. "Good thing I followed you. I knew you'd get into some kind of trouble, bumbling along and…"

Angus grabbed the torch and went to plunge into the darkness after Vanora, but the narrow passageway branched off in two directions. Angus paused and peered down one of the dark, musty tunnels. Chew marks and scratches covered the walls.

"Fine, don't even take a second to thank me," Woodworm huffed.

"Which way?" Angus asked.

Woodworm pointed to a narrow tunnel. "That one leads to their nest. But don't expect me to follow you in there. It's quite disgusting and not at all a proper place for a ghost like me to be."

Angus rushed down the tunnel, trying hard to swallow down the overpowering sense of panic rising into his throat.

"Help!" Vanora's shrill scream echoed from the dark, stinking burrow.

Angus weaved through another series of vile tunnels, each more dank and loathsome than the next. Just when Angus had given up hope of ever seeing Vanora again, he spotted her.

She held a stick of chalk in her hand. Her feet were planted on a crudely drawn chalk cross on the filthy, stone floor. The cross seemed to be holding off the evil vermin. All around, hideous rodents with crooked backs and membranous wings stood on sinewy legs. They walked hunched over, dragging articulated, hairless tails, and sniffing with their narrow, pink snouts. Their ratty, dull brown coats were covered with open, oozing sores.

Angus rushed forward, waving his torch. Something slithered across the back of his neck. He wheeled around and jammed his torch into the rat's hideous face. It let out a shriek that painfully penetrated Angus' eardrums. Saliva dripped from its putrid mouth, simmering like acid as it hit the floor. Its unblinking, black eyes festered with a crusty, yellow film.

A dozen more hulking rats entered the chamber, humming in unison. The strange sound formed a curious sort of music that made Angus sleepy. His legs wobbled like rubber bands. A sensation of swimming in a bubbly, warm pool of water washed over him. His eyes began to close—there was nothing he could do to stop them.

He stood perfectly still as more rats drew closer and closer, until at last they had nearly surrounded him. His shattered mind told him to move, but his legs wouldn't cooperate. One stinking rat lunged, and Angus sank down the wall in a daze.

"Cover your ears!" Vanora shouted to him.

Fighting his own body for control, Angus dropped his torch and slapped his palms to his ears to block out the sounds numbing his brain.

Vanora reached into her pocket and pitched one of the dodo eggs into the corner. The rats scrambled for it. Vanora rushed to Angus' side. She grabbed his hand and tried to drag him away. But more rats surrounded them, attracted by the smell of the broken egg. Vanora dropped to the floor and quickly drew another cross. She got Angus to his feet. They huddled in the middle of the cross while more and more rats slunk forward.

The rodents hummed louder. Angus and Vanora covered their ears. Fane's voice broke into Angus' consciousness. *Listen to me, Angus. Take the chalk from your pocket and draw an iron door on the wall, just as you did once before. Most importantly, make sure it has a handle, so you can open it.*

Won't they just follow me? Angus silently asked.

No, they hate iron. They cannot enter through an iron door.

Angus handed Vanora his eggs and whispered. "When I tell you, I want you to toss these. You have to give me enough time to draw us a way out."

"How? We're surrounded."

"I'll tell you later, just throw the eggs as far from here

as you can." Angus eyed the wall with uncertainty. "Do it now."

Vanora chucked the eggs into a far corner. The rats made so much noise, Angus couldn't hear the eggs hit, but they shattered and stuck to the wall. The yolks, neon yellow globs, slithered toward the floor. The rats scrambled and clawed over one another to get at them.

Angus wrestled the chalk out of his pocket.

One cunning rat, bigger than the rest, peered over his shoulder from his meal. He seemed to realize what Angus was up to. Obviously reluctant to leave the feast, he growled, eyed the eggs once more, then crept near. Its mouth hung slack. Green saliva seeped onto the very tips of Angus' shoes, melting some of the plastic. The rat grunted and then eyed its prey with oozing, pink eyes. Angus took a step back, and the rat sprang.

As he wrenched his face away, the chalk slipped from Angus' hand. He snatched the chalk from the filthy corner it had rolled into and frantically drew a doorway. It had worked once before; hopefully it would work again. Angus sketched a doorknob and wrote 'iron' across the door's front.

A flare of light sent sparks flying along the wall. Angus shielded his eyes from the brilliant beam. Before them, a real door took shape. A heavy, iron door.

Angus gripped the knob and jerked his hand back from the heat. He wrapped his jacket around the knob and pulled open the door. "Come, quick!" he yelled.

The rats crept closer.

Only Vanora's eyes moved. She glanced at Angus, then back at the vermin.

"Hurry!" Angus called.

Finally, she left the safety of the cross and bolted for the door. Halfway there, she stumbled and fell, dropping hard on her knees.

The humming rats were only a few feet away now.

"Run!" Angus shouted.

Vanora jumped to her feet. Again she froze as the menacing rodents closed in on her. If she didn't move fast, they'd have her. Angus didn't want to know—and especially didn't want to see—what they would do. He charged forward, snatched her arm, and yanked her through the open doorway.

He slammed the door. Despite the heavy iron, the hissing of the vile rats came through.

Angus surveyed the massive room.

"Give me the torch."

Vanora handed it to him. The flame made peculiar, skinny shadows dance across the room.

"Looks like a pretty narrow tunnel. But we might as well see where it leads." Angus glanced over his shoulder at the stone wall. "We don't want to go back that way." They headed down the tunnel. "Stay in the center, and don't touch the walls," he added.

They traveled silently for a few minutes, weaving through the tunnel that seemed to curve more and more. They finally came to a large, stone door with a steel handle. There were scratch marks on it as if other creatures, not smart enough to use the handle, had tried to gain entrance.

"Stand back, just in case," Angus said.

Vanora took a step away, and Angus pulled open the

door.

"Whoa, it smells like something died in here." Angus held the door ajar and stuck his torch inside. There were wide shelves containing objects of all kinds. Pieces of material, bits of coral, fishing line, and old coats and hats that looked as if they belonged to very small people. Angus scanned every shelf. The cat statue wasn't there.

"It's not here," Angus said, disappointed.

"Oh no! It has to be! You mean we came all this way for nothing?"

"I guess so. Let me use the eyeglass and see if I can find out what happened and where it might be."

"Good idea."

Angus took out his eyeglass and pointed it into the room. He saw a nasty looking beast with a wrinkled face, pointy ears, and slits for eyes, tucking objects into its pockets and looking around to make sure it wasn't being observed. It reached to the very top shelf and grabbed the cat statue, tucking it inside a burlap bag on its hip.

"Something took it. A horrible-looking creature. It grabbed it and then headed out and down the tunnel. We better go see where it went."

"I hope you're right, Angus. Hope this isn't some kind of trap or something."

"How could it be? No one really knows we're here. At least, not yet."

"Are you sure? How do you really know?"

"I just know, that's all. Come on. Let's get the statue and head home."

Angus held the torch high and hurried down the tunnel, following the path the creature had taken. They rounded a corner to a set of winding steps that led down to another level. When they reached the bottom, they found another curving, skinny tunnel, which was well lit by torches along the walls.

They came to a great expanse covered from floor to ceiling in black and white marble. On the walls, several sets of pictures showed strange-looking men dressed in business suits and polished shoes. They had flat noses, squinty eyes, pointed ears, and wide mouths. They looked very stern and unfriendly. Under each picture was a title such as Governor, Chief Justice, Treasurer, and so forth. Before them, a set of wooden doors led under an archway that read *Hobgoblin Hall.*

"It must have been a hobgoblin that took it," Angus whispered. "Maybe we can sneak in and get it back."

"Yeah, but it couldn't have been a hobgoblin you saw. I mean, they are known to be fairly harmless. In fact, they are rumored to be of great help around the house. I think we should go in and ask them."

"How do you know they're friendly?"

"I don't. But it's worth a shot, isn't it? They might be able to tell us where the statue is. Or give it to us, if they have it."

"I hope you're right." Angus grabbed a large metal knocker and tapped it against the door. The sound boomed inside the room, creating a loud, ringing echo. Angus winced. He hadn't meant to knock so loud.

"Enter," commanded a booming voice.

Angus pushed on the stone doors, and they headed inside. The meeting hall was filled with hobgoblins sitting on a dozen or more wooden benches. At the head of the room sat a large desk with a stern-looking hobgoblin sitting behind it. He appeared very old and crabby. He wore a white, curly wig and a long, black gown, and he clutched a gavel in his hand. Angus couldn't believe the length of the creature's fingernails. He shivered at the amount of hair on the backs of the creature's hands.

The old hobgoblin leaned forward and scowled. "What is the meaning of this? How did you get here?"

Angus' heart jumped and skittered around in his chest. He cleared his throat. "I'm Angus MacBain, sir. I'm here because I need assistance."

The hob's face tightened; his eyes grew wide. He reached into the desk drawer and slipped on a pair of wire spectacles.

"A MacBain? Heir to the throne?"

"Yes, sir."

"Please step forward and approach the council," the hob said.

Vanora squeezed Angus' arm. "Good luck. I'll wait here."

"Thanks." Angus stepped forward and stood in front of the massive desk. The hobgoblin peered at him over his glasses.

"Yes, sir, I…"

The hobgoblin leaned forward and scowled down at Angus. "Please address me as Your Honor."

Angus nodded and cleared his throat. "Your Honor, are you familiar with Fane Vargovic?"

The creature's jaw tightened. "We know him well. Fane Vargovic is a respected advisor to the MacBain kings."

"Something terrible has happened to him. He's trapped and will die if I don't help him." Angus could hardly get the words out.

The hobgoblin raised his hand. "We are aware of his plight."

The hall erupted in a commotion of whispers and hissing voices. The Hobgoblin banged a gavel down on the desktop. "Quiet! *BE QUIET*!" The creature focused on Angus. "Continue."

"We need to find an object—a twin to the one that was stolen. One that will keep Fane from aging. It's a statue of Tarvish, King MacBain's wildcat."

"We know what it is."

"You do? How did you know?"

"We know all dark things that Lord Dragomir does. Word travels quickly in these cavern walls."

"Tell me where it is—please!" Angus replied quickly.

"It will do no good to tell you. It's impossible to retrieve now."

"Please, just tell me! I have a right to know, even if it's beyond my grasp."

"As you wish." The hobgoblin cleared his throat. "It's in the hands of great evil. The motive behind it is twofold—to free Lord Dragomir, and to kill the wizard Fane. You see, when you trapped Dragomir, his followers banded together to figure out what the object was that allowed Fane to travel between worlds and where it had been hidden. They did this to destroy Fane so he could no longer help you. Also, once Fane was dead, the gateway would be open for every cursed creature, imprisoned in this place at the king's request, to escape. They would then enter the human world and destroy all that is good. They would also travel to Ceòban and cause harm as well. Fane is the only one who can keep the gateway closed. There is nothing to do now. Fane will die, and so will all of us. It is just the way it is."

Fearful cries and shouting echoed in the great hall.

"Why won't you at least tell me and let me try?"

"I cannot tell you, because I have taken an oath not to risk the life of the last of the MacBain kings. It is against the rules."

"What do rules matter if we're all dead?"

The hall erupted in a mixture of shouting voices. "Tell him!" someone screamed. "You must save Fane Vargovic!" called another. "Without Fane, all will be lost!" The voices rose in pitch, growing louder and louder. "*TELL HIM!*" they chanted in unison.

The hob banged his gavel down again. "All right, all right," he yelled. "I will tell you, but be warned—it is at your own risk. The object you seek is with the trows, in their great and terrible towers in the belly of this cave. Trows, as you may or may not know, are a dark race of Goblinoids. They are our evil cousins, and they take delight in stealing when they can—they've taken many items from those who dwell here. As creatures of the night, Trows prefer to make their home in the deepest part of this cave. Sunlight is their enemy. If caught in it, they become frozen like statues until the sun goes down. Trows are nearly impossible to contend with because they thrive in the blackness, making burrows in the deep gloom. Their home is not entirely by their choice—Trows were cast out and cursed to remain in darkness for all time for their evil deeds of cannibalism upon humankind. They have formed a kingdom called Trow Towers—rumored to be a dangerous and confusing lair made of stolen gold and human bones—but no one has ever returned to confirm this.

Angus looked back at Vanora, whose eyes were wide and face pale.

"And you are sure they're the ones who have the cat?" Angus asked.

"Yes, of course! The cat is their bargaining tool. They want to use it to invade humankind. They want Fane dead because then they can be free. The curse he placed on them would be broken upon his death, and they could return to the dark forests."

"How do we get to Trow Towers?"

"You go out the way you came and take the first door you come to. You will have to journey down many steps and through many doorways. You will see signs along your way. Take great care." The hobgoblin paused, reached into his desk, and pulled out a very flat and thin piece of folded paper. "Take this map. It will guide you to where you need to go and hopefully steer you away from any harm—if that's possible in such a dreadful place."

Angus reached for the map, and the hobgoblin grabbed Angus' arm. The creature's thick fingernails bit into his skin. "Take great care that you follow the directions this map provides," the hobgoblin said. "If you veer off the trail—even for a second—you will surely die."

Angus nodded, and the hob slowly released him, staring into Angus' eyes.

"Good luck to you," he said. "You will certainly need

it."

"Thanks." Angus turned to leave.

"Wait," the hobgoblin said. "Have you given any thought to how you will stop it from being stolen again? Now that everyone knows what the object is, there will be more dark ones coming to steal it again."

"I have no idea. Guess I didn't think that far ahead because I was so focused on just finding it. What can I do?"

"You will need to see a powerful spell-caster. Someone who can cement it to the island for good. There is only one who is powerful enough to do that—a sea witch who despises Dragomir. She lives in the darkest and dampest regions of this cave. You must visit her after you get the statue from the trows—if you survive, that is."

Angus tucked the map into his front pocket and turned to leave. Behind him, rows of hobgoblins gaped at him. Some sneered, while others wrung their hands nervously. They stepped aside, bowing as he walked through the cleared path to Vanora. He didn't know if he should bow back to them or if he should say something. He simply nodded his thanks and left as quickly as he could with Vanora.

"Did you hear what he said about the Trows being cannibals?" Vanora paused and lowered her voice. "I've read about them being evil—but I've never heard of them eating flesh! What are we going to do? You don't even have your sword or shield."

"I know. I think you should wait here for me. It isn't fair of me to ask you to risk your life as well as mine."

"No. I won't let you go alone. I told you that before,

Angus."

Angus paused and took Vanora's hand. "I know how you feel. I know you want to stick with me to help, but it doesn't make sense that both of us should be put in danger. I can't take the thought of something happening to you."

Vanora rushed into Angus' arms. He held her tight. She smelled like vanilla and cherry lip balm. He liked the way it made the crazy world stop spinning, even if only for a few seconds.

She pulled away and peered into his face. "I have to go with you, Angus. I'll go crazy waiting here. I have to do it for my dad. Please."

Angus looked away.

Vanora took his hand. "Please, Angus. I insist on going."

"All right." He sighed. "I understand why you want to go. I just wish things could be easier and less dangerous. It's hard looking after both of us."

"I know that, Angus, but I can help too. I'm not a child. I know a lot about the creatures from my dad, or I've read about them someplace. And I know how to deal with most of them."

"You're totally right. You do help a lot. It's just that I hate for both of us to have to risk our lives. I guess you're right. We better get going before it gets any later."

They hurried through a series of tunnels and down staircases until they entered into a wide area marked with a caution sign.

Vanora pointed to a large, round door. "Look, there it is!"

Written across the door was a large wooden sign that said *LAST CHANCE—TURN BACK NOW*. On the bottom of the sign, someone had scrawled something else.

Angus looked closer, reading the words aloud. "Beware! Danger! Enter at your own risk."

9

Entrance into the Unknown

Angus tugged hard on the handle, and the door groaned open. They walked inside. Two glowing torches on the wall lit the entryway. When Angus took a step forward, he felt something bang on his toe. Angus looked down, and to his surprise, he saw a mouse holding a long steel pike. He waved it at Angus, backing him up into Vanora.

"What are you doing?" Vanora asked.

"There's a rat… or… something," Angus said, pointing at the miniscule rodent in tiny body armor, with a pointy nose and whiskers.

"A rat? *A rat?*" the creature squeaked. "Can't you see I'm a *mouse*?"

"Uh… what do you want?"

"You must pay the fare in order to pass," the mouse huffed. "Descendent of a king or not—everyone must pay the fare."

"Wait a second… how did you know I was a…"

"Everyone knows you're here by now." The mouse lowered its voice and nodded toward the entrance. "Especially the dark ones; they've been whispering about you all day. That's why I must insist on collecting the fare now."

Vanora planted her hands on her hips. "What fare?"

The mouse sighed, leaning on his metal staff. "Word has spread of your quest, and, as far as a fare goes, everyone pays when they journey beyond this point. It's a lot of work cleaning up the carnage. You can imagine how blood stains the old rockwork. Then we have to hire a cleanup crew, a mortician, and a stonemason. It's quite costly. The fare pays for any messy accidents that occur." He pulled out a comically large business card, which read *Death and Dismemberment Cleanup Incorporated.*

Vanora glanced at Angus, wide-eyed, before turning back to the mouse. "Does anyone ever come back for a refund?"

The creature rubbed his whiskers, then screwed up his face, thinking. "Can't say anyone ever has. Not in the three hundred years that I've worked at this post."

"Three hundred years!" Vanora exclaimed.

"Never mind that," Angus said. "How much is the fee?"

"Depends."

"On what?" Angus asked.

"On the size of those who journey here, of course." The mouse rubbed his chin. "Big fellow like you would cost a pretty penny. I'll have to get my measuring stick." The mouse squinted at Vanora. "She'd be less expensive, of course. I'd say around ten pounds of fairy dust."

"Fairy dust?" Angus said. "We don't have any fairy

dust. Will you take something else?"

"Well, you can sign a form that says we get to keep your teeth… if we can find them, that is."

"Gross!" Vanora said. "Why would you want someone's teeth?"

"Why not?" the mouse replied. "Teeth are valuable items, you know—especially for those who don't have them. And of course, hags will buy them for a good price to sell at the floating market."

Angus looked at Vanora. "Want to sign away your, um… teeth? I guess I don't mind."

"That depends—what if we survive?" Vanora narrowed her eyes at the mouse. "Will you still want our teeth then?"

The little creature chuckled. "No, of course not. Not in that case, because there would be no need for cleanup. But then again, no one's ever survived—not that I've ever heard of."

"Okay," Angus said. "Then it's a deal. Give me whatever I need to sign."

The mouse took out a tiny notepad and handed Angus an ink pen that was so small Angus had a hard time holding on to it.

The mouse pointed to several places. "Just put your X there, and then again here."

Angus did as he was told.

"Okay, young lady. Now it's your turn." The mouse held the notebook as Vanora signed.

The rodent tucked the notebook away and then took a long look at them. "I wish you luck," he said, letting out a sad sigh. "Such a shame to see young people lose their lives. Sure you won't change your mind?"

Angus shook his head. "Wish we could, but we don't have much of a choice."

"I'm sure sorry about that. Maybe somehow you'll make it out alive. You never know." The mouse turned to leave, and then paused. "Just one more thing." He lowered his voice to nearly a whisper, forcing Angus and Vanora to lean forward and strain to hear him. "Beware of the other evil things that dwell down there. There are many that want revenge for what you did to the dark one. They still serve him, even here. Lots of lost souls."

Angus' throat went dry. "We will. Thanks."

The rodent eyed Angus. "I see you've come unarmed?"

Angus nodded. "My mother put my sword and shield away for safekeeping while I'm at school for the winter."

"Then you'll be needing something to fend off the evil ones. Otherwise, you will have no chance at all against the dark spirits." The mouse scurried off and returned with a basket filled with trinkets. "Let me see what I can recommend." The mouse smiled and pulled out a series of smooth, white objects, laying them on the floor.

"What are they?" Angus asked.

"Shells, of course!"

"Seashells?" asked Vanora. "How can shells protect us?"

The mouse shook its head. "You human folk never cease to surprise me with your ignorance."

"Hey!" Vanora exclaimed.

Angus held up his hand. "Please, tell us what we need to know."

"There are several shells that can be used for protection.

But you will have to select only one. Magical sea creatures have a special creed. They never collect more than they need. Fairly take and fairly give, that's their motto. I'll have to take something from you to give to the sea in payment of what you've been given."

"So what are our choices? Looks like there are a lot of shells to choose from."

"They all protect in different ways. This one, for example…" The mouse picked up a small brown shell. "This is a Clusterwink shell. It comes from a small sea snail, which is usually found clinging to rocks at the shoreline. They send out blasts of green light and are excellent at frightening off predators of flight and at providing light for dark journeys." The mouse picked up another shell. "Clam shells, like this one, are good for comforting and healing. And as there are many shells to pick from, may I make a suggestion?"

Angus nodded. "Yes, of course."

The mouse carefully tucked the other shells away. He reached into a side pocket of the basket and pulled out a large conch shell. "Even though this is a common seashell, many people are not aware of its uses." He handed it to Angus. "Put this in your pocket and keep it close. If you put the shell to your lips and blow, the power of the sacred sea will dissolve most winged creatures—things that do not dwell in the sea. Blood-sucking bats are a staple of the trow diet. I suspect the closer you get to Trow Towers, the more trouble you will have with them. They can be unrelenting, especially when they encounter fresh blood."

"Eww," Vanora said. "Gross."

"Thank you, but there's one problem," Angus said. "You said we had to have something to give back to the ocean?"

"Yes, that's right."

"We don't have anything to give."

The mouse frowned and rubbed his whiskers.

"Wait!" Vanora exclaimed. "How about my pink earrings—they're made of coral."

"Oh, that would be a fine gift!" The mouse beamed.

Vanora took off the earrings and handed them to him. "Here you go."

"Thank you! Good luck to you!" The mouse scooped up his basket and left without saying another word.

Vanora frowned. "He left rather quickly. Hope this wasn't some kind of a scam."

"Yeah, me too. By the sounds of it, we need all the help we can get. I hope the shell really works. Actually, I hope we just don't need it," Angus replied. "We have enough to deal with besides blood-sucking bats."

10

TROW TOWERS

Angus gripped the handrail and leaned over the edge. A stone staircase spiraled downward into the darkness far below. Each step was rough and misshapen and looked to be very old—perhaps even ancient. The staircase was covered in dust as if it hadn't been used for a very long time. Angus could understand why no one would want to venture into the far reaches of this place. It was unsettling how dark it was and how overgrown the moss was on each step—not to mention the handrail covered in cobwebs.

As Angus peered downward, a strange scuttling and shuffling sound echoed.

"Did you hear that?" Angus asked.

"Hear what?"

Angus leaned farther over the edge, listening. Everything remained quiet. "I thought I heard something."

Vanora paled. "I hope it wasn't whispering. Remember what the mouse said about the dark ones talking about you?"

Angus nodded. "It wasn't whispering I heard. It sounded like shuffling feet or footsteps."

Vanora swallowed hard. "I suppose this place makes lots of weird echoes and noises. After all, most caves do—don't they?"

Angus raised his eyebrows. "I guess so, but not like that…"

"We must be crazy for going down there. Anything could be hiding in the dark, waiting to attack us." Vanora stared at the winding steps. "It looks so creepy. Did you notice how those steps seem like they go on forever?"

Angus nodded. "And they're covered in slippery moss, so be careful." Angus started down the steps. He gripped the scaly handrail, hoping he wouldn't lose his footing.

Vanora followed close behind. Her foot slipped, and she pitched forward, colliding with Angus.

Angus' feet slipped out from under him. He grabbed the handrail with both hands. When he regained his footing, he looked over his shoulder at Vanora. "Watch out. You've got to hold on to the railing, or you're going to kill us both."

"Sorry. I *was* holding on, but it's so slick that it's hard to stay upright."

Their soggy footsteps echoed into the darkness until finally the moss on the steps seemed to thin out. In place of the moss were tiny pools of yellow water and fat beetles that scuttled out of the way. The farther they traveled, the brighter the moss on the walls glowed, providing light along the way.

A strange, high-pitched cry erupted somewhere below

them. It was a mournful cry, as if something were in terrible pain.

Vanora clutched Angus' arm. "Did you hear that? What was it?"

"I'm not sure." Angus paused. "It's probably one of those horrible wraiths."

"Better keep your eyeglass handy."

Angus fumbled for it in his pocket. He pulled it out and studied it. "It's not glowing, so whatever it is isn't close by."

"Thank goodness!"

"We'll keep going, and if it starts to glow then we'll know we have something to worry about. Until then, let's do the best we can and try to keep calm and relaxed."

"I hope you're joking. No way could I relax in this place."

"Whatever; just concentrate on each step and try not to worry."

"It's hard to stay focused. I just hope we're going in the right direction. I feel like we're running out of time for my dad, and it worries me."

"We can only do the best we can. Right?"

Vanora nodded. "Yep, no matter what, at least we can say we tried."

The stairs snaked into a spiral, dividing into two separate staircases. One set turned upward at a sharp angle, and one turned downward.

"Wow, which way do we go?" Vanora asked.

"Let me look at the map the hobgoblins gave me." Angus pulled it from his shirt pocket. Everything on the map appeared three-dimensional and it glowed a brilliant green. Angus frowned. "It doesn't show it."

"Wait!" Vanora pointed to an arrow on the map. Words materialized. They floated across the page. "There—look! *This way to Trow Towers*."

"Wow, that's so cool! And there we are!" Angus pointed to two stick-like figures on the map. Soon the figures started to take more shape. Angus lifted his hand and waved, and one of the figures on the map waved back.

Vanora rubbed her eyes. "It's amazing! At least we won't lose our way."

Angus nodded. "I sure hope not." He gently folded the map and slipped it back into his pocket.

They took the steps on their left, which twisted around a few turns and then descended sharply.

"Hang on," Angus said. "It's getting steeper. Watch your footing."

The moss glowed brighter along the path, lighting the way. At times, Angus caught glimpses of other staircases going up and down, and other openings and passageways in the walls. It was a confusing honeycomb of chasms and burrows. If he didn't keep his attention on the path, Angus feared he would never remember the way out.

The trail led past a large grotto. Strange cries rose like flames from the gloomy place.

"That must be where the wailing sounds were coming from," Vanora whispered. "What do you think is down there?"

"Something horrible, I imagine."

Angus took out his eyeglass and pointed it into the dark hole. He made out a village with crude dwellings covered in moss, and slime surrounded an eroded palace.

The castle walls wept with the ever-present damp. Clumps of mushrooms clung to the cut stones, and snails with brilliant green shells made snotty tracks across the window frames.

"It's a city, a creepy one."

A terrible, ear-splitting shriek shook Angus to the core. A light from the eyeglass suddenly went on, sending a bright beam of light into the murky place, penetrating the darkest of its regions. Angry cries rose from far below.

"Oh, no!" Vanora screamed. "It must be a city of wraiths!"

Hooded figures boiled out of the houses, swooping upward and screeching in rage. They flew over Angus and Vanora's heads, swirling in tight corners. Their piercing screams tore into Angus' brain, until he could hardly think. He aimed the eyeglass, sending shards of light through them. Several fell to the ground and disintegrated, while others retreated into the dark city from where they came.

One large wraith continued to circle around them. It looked different than the others. There was something more menacing about it. Its eyes burned crimson, its long, black robe fluttered about it. Every time Angus tried to hit it with the light from the eyeglass, the creature darted just out of the way.

"Oh, no!" Vanora exclaimed.

"What is it?"

"I've read about these. It's a blood wraith! See its red eyes? They are nearly invincible. They cause death by internal bleeding. They can produce wounds just by looking at you!"

Angus tried to hit it again with the light, but it bounced easily out of the way, flying to the other side of the cave and then circling them.

"I can't seem to hit it with the light—it's too fast," Angus yelled. Before he could say another word, a heavy stream of blood flowed from his nose.

"Angus, kill it! Hurry, it's making you bleed!"

Angus held out the eyeglass, this time aiming quickly to the left of the blood wraith. The specter slipped to the side and was hit dead center. The wraith exploded, sending blood splattering over Angus and Vanora.

Vanora wiped her eyes and mouth. "Yuck!"

Angus rubbed his hands across his T-shirt and then used the underside of it to wipe his nose and face. "At least it's dead. Thank goodness." He took out the map. "Looks like we need to keep going straight ahead. Let's hurry and get out of here."

They continued onward, traveling through musty tunnels with walls crawling with slugs, beetles, and fat cockroaches the size of rats. The path led along narrow passageways that seemed to go on forever and then spider out in all directions.

Without the map to guide them, they would have never found their way.

They passed by dank and festering tunnels and through puffs of eerie fog that filtered into their pathway like cotton balls. They passed wooden doorways and crooked windows that opened to reveal solid rock walls. Sometimes the trail beneath their feet seemed to disappear in a heavy mist, only to reappear again when they stopped walking. Strange circles, carved here and there in the walls, seemed to swirl, making it hard to keep their balance.

After traveling for what felt like an eternity, Angus and Vanora entered into an enormous cavern. Torches made of moss glowed along the walls, emitting a terrible stench that burned Angus' nose and sensitive eyes. Massive stone figures skulked down at them with hate-filled expressions.

"Wow," Angus said. "They look so mean! And check out those sloped foreheads, flat faces and pointy ears… they look really different."

"And little slits for eyes, and wicked, sharp fangs!"

Each figure wore a thick suit of armor. Their long arms hung almost to the ground, with clawed and hairy fingers. In their right hands, they clutched battleaxes and in the left, sharp spears.

Angus read aloud from the map, "*War Memorial to Fallen Trows.*"

"So, it's like a shrine. A place to honor those who died in battle."

Angus nodded. "Looks like it."

Angus ventured farther into the room with Vanora on his heels. They came across altars and chairs made of thick, sloped skulls and crooked leg bones. More piles of bones made up other furnishings. Some of the bones appeared to be human, while others were odd and misshapen, belonging to unknown beasts.

Vanora walked closer and studied the odd-shaped remains. "Just look at the gnaw marks on those strange-looking bones. What kind of creature do you think they belonged to?"

Angus shuddered. "Probably their own kind. Remember what the hobgoblin said about them being cannibals."

Vanora shivered. "I don't want to think about it."

"You're right. Let's keep going."

"Which way?"

Angus took out his map again. "Looks like we need to travel directly south through this place, into another cavern, and then over a tall, stone bridge.

Vanora gripped Angus' arm. "I'm worried about this. These creatures seemed to have thrived down here. I mean, if you look at their faces, they have adapted pretty well. Their eyes are small and narrow for seeing in the dark, and their flat noses must give them a better sense of smell. I bet they can travel pretty fast with those long arms and clawed hands. They probably crawl into all sorts of holes to hide and watch for prey."

"I'm sure you're right. Keep a sharp eye out—just in case."

Vanora nervously looked around her. "We should keep going. This place is too open. They could even be watching us now."

Angus and Vanora quickly left the Trow Memorial behind and passed into another cavern with branching tunnels. They hiked sharply uphill, over large, flat stones worn smooth and thin. The sides of the trail gave way to sharp drop-offs into the dark on both sides. Angus paused and looked down; he didn't like the idea of climbing so high. He peered downward, and everything started to spin; his head felt funny.

"Angus, are you okay?" Vanora lunged to keep Angus

from falling, hitting her toe on a rock. Angus grabbed her arm just as she pitched forward and nearly went over the ledge.

Angus pulled her to her feet. "Are *you* okay?"

Vanora struggled to catch her breath. She bent over and planted her hands on her knees. "Wow, for a second I really thought I was done for."

"Me too."

Vanora stood upright. "Let's keep going. Looks like it gets a lot steeper ahead."

Angus nodded. "And darker, too."

They hiked up the stone path that rose like a wave before them, until they reached the top. Then the terrain evened out, and they reached the foot of a narrow, wooden bridge. The structure was suspended in darkness.

"Do you think the ropes and boards are still okay?" Vanora asked.

Angus started over the bridge. "I guess we'll find out."

Below them, the sound of water could be heard. With each step, the bridge shifted beneath their feet, and a cracking sound could be heard.

"Be really careful," Angus said. "You never know what's down there."

"What do you think is in the water?"

"I don't know, and to be honest I really don't want to think about it."

When they reached the end of the bridge, they entered into another series of caverns. Angus was glad to be on stable ground again.

A shuffling sound came from behind them; sharp voices hissed.

Angus' heart leapt. "Who's there?"

The voices dropped away. Silence filled the air. All Angus could hear was his own breath sawing in and out and the pounding of blood in his ears.

From his pocket, the eyeglass suddenly beamed.

"Oh no!" Vanora squealed. She looked around nervously. "Do you think it's blood wraiths again?"

"I don't know. Stay right behind me," Angus said.

The eyeglass glowed brighter.

Vanora clutched his arm. "Whatever it is, it's getting closer!"

They crept forward and around a sharp corner. In the middle of the path stood a cloaked phantom with its back to them. Angus stopped short and stood protectively in front of Vanora. The ghost turned slowly. Its face resembled rotting leather, with eyes sunken deep into its skeletal head. So deep, in fact, that even the light from the eyeglass failed to reach them. The ghost was skinnier than the wraiths they had encountered earlier, and from beneath its dark robes came a strange flapping. The phantom opened its mouth wide and let out a long, horrible screech.

Angus nearly dropped the eyeglass to cover his ears.

The ghost spread its skinny arms and dissolved into a hundred black bats. The bats hovered for a moment, and all at once they turned and flew directly at them.

"Run!" Angus yelled.

The bats descended on them, tearing at their hair and clothes. They hurried down the steps, fighting to get away. The bats were unrelenting. They dove at Angus' head and twisted their feet into Vanora's hair.

"Use the shell!" Vanora yelled.

"What?"

"The shell!"

A hot surge of adrenaline rushed into Angus' veins. He had forgotten all about the conch shell. He fumbled for it and almost dropped it as the bats swooped into his face, clawing and tearing at the tender skin near his swollen eyes. Somehow, Angus managed to get the shell to his lips. He blew hard as the bats scratched at his hands to stop him. The shell made a low pitch that vibrated off the walls of the cave.

The bats flew back and then, bit by bit, dissolved into piles of black ash on the stone floor. Angus rushed to the messy pile on the cave floor. He wanted to kick it and scatter it around so the bats couldn't reform, but before he could the ash swirled into the air and disappeared.

Vanora bent over, resting her hands on her knees. "What was that thing?" she gasped.

Angus shook his head, fighting to catch his breath. "I don't know. Some kind of bat-ghoul thing. How should I know? I just hope it doesn't come back." Angus tucked the shell into his pocket. "At least we know what works to get rid of it."

Vanora nodded. "Yeah, thank goodness."

"We better keep moving. With all the noise we've made, I'm sure every ghost, ghoul, and creepy creature knows we're here."

Vanora nodded, her gaze darting around the room. "I know. It's just so nerve-racking never knowing what we'll run into. How much longer do you think it is to the Trows?"

"I'm not sure because I can't tell how to judge distance on the map. All we can do is just keep going and try to be quieter."

"Can you imagine how horrible the Trows must be?" Vanora said.

"Anything that lives down here has to be."

"To be honest, I'm scared to death, Angus. But I keep thinking about my dad and about Fane, and it keeps me going."

Angus nodded. "Me too. But fear isn't a protection; it's something we have to overcome if we're going to get the statue. I'm hoping I can sneak in and steal it before they know what happened."

"I don't know, Angus. It has to be heavily guarded. No way are they just going to let us waltz in there and take it from them."

"I guess we'll find out, won't we?"

Vanora nodded. "Unfortunately."

They continued onward, passing through dark caverns slick with slime, deep crevices cold as ice, and thick, stone walls, glowing with green fungus to guide them. Moss, gravel, and sand rolled beneath their feet and caused them to lose their footing. Angus plunged deeper into the tunnel. He hoped they'd find the towers soon; though what he would do when that happened, he had no idea. How in the world could he get the statue away from the Trows? If only he had brought his shield and sword or even a torch to guide them. Just as he feared, the glowing fungus on the rock walls faded as they traveled deeper and deeper in the belly of the cave.

Angus took out the eyeglass, hoping it would help. But

all he saw were figures in the dark that made him jump. When the fungus covering the walls grew sparse and the darkness was complete, they had to feel their way along the walls.

"Are you sure we're going the right way?" Vanora asked.

Angus took out the map the hobgoblins had given him. Vanora held on to one edge while they examined it. It glowed brightly in the dark. Everything on the map seemed to be moving.

"Look!" Vanora pointed. "There we are."

Angus squinted. Two objects holding a large sheet of paper were outlined in glowing green.

Words formed in the center of the map in a misty haze. *You're going the right way.*

"That's comforting, at least," Vanora said.

"Look!" Angus said. The map showed wispy figures just behind them on the path. "Wraiths! Lots of them. Does that mean they're following us?"

"I don't know." Vanora swallowed hard. "I hope not."

A cry erupted in the darkness surrounding them. The eyeglass blazed into a brilliant beam of light that illuminated the entire ceiling from Angus' pocket.

Vanora gasped. "We have to get out of here!"

Angus shoved the map into his pocket and grabbed Vanora's hand. "Come on!"

They ran, struggling to find their way through the dark tunnel with the wraiths shrieking and chasing after them. They ducked into a narrow crevice in the cave wall. The wraiths floated over the stone floor as relentless as death. They endlessly searched, traveling back and forth, swirling and screeching their fury into the darkness.

Angus grabbed the eyeglass and pointed it at them. The wraiths shrieked and shrank away from the light.

"Stay here." Angus left Vanora in the crevice and stepped forward, pushing the wraiths toward the back of the cave wall. There were so many of them Angus didn't know which one to fight first.

They attacked from all sides. Angus swirled the light in a circle, hitting several of them at once. He sliced the light through the air, destroying several more. One wraith swept into the crevice and pulled Vanora from her hiding place. Before she could get away, it gripped her by the throat and lifted her off her feet. She kicked and clawed at the ghostly hand, but the wraith only flew higher, soaring all the way to the top of the cave wall.

"Let her go!" Angus yelled. Before he could aim the light at it, another one swooped behind him, knocking him off his feet.

The eyeglass spun out of his grasp. One of the wraiths dove for it, reaching out with its clawed hand to steal the object. Angus got to his feet and ran at the creature full on. He passed straight through it and grabbed the eyeglass.

A bone-stabbing chill raced into Angus. A bitter cold like he had never experienced penetrated every cell in his body. Icy fingers took hold of his throat. He struggled to breath. It was like being immersed in artic waters. Angus' head pounded, and pain seared into his temples with every rapid beat of his racing heart. Something warm and sticky trickled from his ears and ran from his nose—blood! Pointing the eyeglass at a large blood wraith,

Angus stepped forward, more determined than ever to find the wraith that held Vanora.

As the blood wraith in front of him exploded from the eyeglass' light, Angus spotted Vanora. She was being held by another blood wraith, this one skinner and smaller than the one that had held him. Blood trickled from Vanora's nose, and her eyes bugged out of her head. Her mouth fell open, and her face turned purple. She couldn't breathe! If he didn't do something soon, the wraith would kill her.

Angus lunged forward, aiming the eyeglass at the creature. The wraith shrieked in pain but held on, determined to get its revenge. Angus' head throbbed and his eyes burned as the blood wraith stared him down. He kept on with the eyeglass until the wraith exploded and Vanora fell to the floor, unmoving.

Angus wanted to run to her, but more wraiths bore down on him. He turned in a circle, cutting down several more. Only a few thin ones remained. They seemed weaker than the others. Angus ran toward them, eyeglass extended.

They huddled together for a moment, and as he advanced with the light they vaporized, disappearing into cracks and fissures in the stone wall.

Angus ran to Vanora and dropped to his knees. He cradled her head, wiping away the blood from her mouth, and eased her up from the floor. Her eyes were closed, and her body was limp. "Vanora! Can you hear me? Are you okay?"

She moaned and cracked open one eye. "Angus?" she whispered. "Are they gone?"

"Yes, but I'm sure they'll be back. We need to keep going. Can you walk?"

Vanora nodded. "Just give me a minute. I feel so weak. It was sucking the blood right out of my veins."

"Are you sure you're okay? Should we go back?"

"No, Angus! Not after we've come so far. I'll be okay. Just a little headache, that's all."

Vanora got to her feet, but her legs shook. She steadied herself and then brushed off her shorts. She leaned against the cave wall for a moment with an odd expression on her face.

"Are you sure you're okay?"

Vanora nodded. "You want to know something? As weird as it sounds, I wish my dad could have seen those creatures. I mean, I told him a lot of what we encountered on our last journey, but someday I want him to see for himself. I want him to know he isn't crazy, like so many people think, just because he believes in things that aren't of this world."

Angus nodded. "I totally get that. Not everyone can be open-minded. So often, people close their minds to things they can't see or feel. If you ask me, they're the ones who are crazy."

"We better get going." Vanora wiped at her eyes.

Angus started down the trail. "Don't worry, your dad is going to be all right, and maybe someday we can bring him here and show him everything."

Vanora nodded and followed Angus. "I hope so. Not that I really ever want to come back to Trow Towers…"

"I know the feeling. But don't worry. Everything is going to work out. I'm sure of it." Angus wished he could believe his own words, but he knew the dangers that lay ahead. Although he was grateful for the eyeglass, he longed for his sword and shield. How would they make it back out alive with only an eyeglass to protect them? There were so many creatures lying in wait for their return that it all seemed hopeless. Maybe he could find another way out instead. He could only hope.

Tense as they were, they traveled in silence and followed the map, on the constant lookout for wraiths and other creatures.

Vanora let out a defeated sigh and glanced at her watch. "We've been walking for over an hour, and we still don't seem to be any closer."

Angus leaned against the wall. "We can rest for a few minutes, then we have to keep going. I feel like my feet are going to burst into flames."

Vanora giggled, and Angus smiled. It was comforting to hear her laughter. They hadn't even managed to reach the Trows, and already he was exhausted. How would he ever have the strength to battle them?

Angus shook off his doubts and pressed forward. They hurried as fast as they could, slipping here and there on the spongy moss growing in the cracks of the stone floor. They threaded their way among the stalagmites and stalactites, coming at last to two passages branching off in opposite directions. Though the map said they should take the passage farthest to the right, the one in the center had a pile of rocks with a little, wooden sign that said *Shortcut to Trow Towers*.

Angus nudged Vanora. "Look! A shortcut."

Vanora smirked and studied the sign. "I'm not buying

it."

"What do you mean?"

"Check out the writing." Vanora pointed to the sign. "It's totally different than the others—it looks like someone or something scrawled it out with a dull blade. The letters are all uneven and crooked. It has to be a trap."

Angus studied both entrances. "But what if it isn't? What if it really *is* a shortcut? It could save us a lot of time. All the other signs have pointed us in the right direction, so why not take a chance on this one?"

"Because it might get us into trouble, that's why."

Angus sighed in frustration. "What do you suggest, then?"

"I think we should stick with the map. What does it say? Can I see it?"

Angus handed the map to Vanora.

Vanora took the map and carefully examined it. She studied several spots, and then suddenly her face lit up. "Look!" She pointed with an index finger. "It shows us standing near the sign, but there's an arrow pointing us in the opposite direction. I think it's wise to stick with the way the map shows."

"Even so… what if this way saves us a ton of time? I think I should at least take a look and see where it goes."

"I don't know, Angus… it seems risky."

"Well, then stay here. I'll go check it out and be right back."

"I don't think that's wise, Angus. What if you don't come back? I don't want to be stuck here all alone."

"I won't be gone long, I promise. Okay?"

"I don't know. Like I said before, I think we should

stick with the map."

"Give me five minutes. I just wanna take a peek."

Before Vanora could protest, Angus crept halfway into the tunnel. The moss was sparse, so there wasn't much light to guide the way. Ahead, Angus thought he spotted a flicker of light. From somewhere deep inside, he heard and the sound of shuffling feet. He waited several seconds to see if someone or something emerged. From every dark corner, Angus felt eyes watching him. Angus hurried back the way he came. Something behind him shuffled, and Angus paused, searching the darkness. He waited a few more seconds, then whirled around to leave, when he bumped into Vanora.

"Oops, sorry."

"What did you see? Anything?"

"No, but there's someone or something else in here. You were right about this place. We gotta get out of here, and fast."

Before Angus could say another word, rocks tumbled down from all directions, trapping them in the dark tunnel. Angus shielded Vanora with his body as boulders of all shapes and sizes hammered down around them. They dodged the larger ones, but smaller bits of rock and dirt peppered them like missiles. A cloud of dust rose and mixed with the stench of disintegrating moss. Angus found it hard to breathe, coughing and hacking, until finally, the dust settled. He let Vanora loose from his grip.

"See, I told you it was a trap!" She coughed long and hard before regaining her voice. "How will we ever get out of here?"

Angus shrugged. "I have no clue. I should have listened

to you. I'm sorry."

"Forget it. It's too late to be sorry now. We need to focus on finding a way out. I'm trying not to panic and freak out, but I have claustrophobia—I hate dark spaces."

"Me too."

"Check the map, and see if it will show us a way."

Angus carefully unfolded the map. In the darkness, words glowed like fire from the map. *Danger! Return to the main path!*

"This isn't good. We can't get back to the main path because it's obviously blocked." Angus paused and looked around in the darkness. "There doesn't seem to be any way out now."

"What are we going to do, then?"

Angus folded the map and slipped it back into his pocket. He inched forward, pulling Vanora along with him. Carefully, he made his way down the tunnel. Maybe he could find a loose stone or somehow find another way out. His eyes watered from the damp, musty odor. He reached out to steady himself along the rock wall; when he touched slime, he jerked his hand back.

"What if there's no way out?" Vanora said.

"I don't know, but I'll figure it out," Angus said.

Angus' gut churned with the idea of being trapped in the dark forever. If only Fane was here to guide him. Something shuffled to the right of them.

Vanora grabbed onto Angus's arm. "What was that?"

Angus squinted in the dark. "I don't know; I heard that same sound before."

The shuffling noise sounded again. Vanora gasped. "It's getting closer."

"Come on and help me," Angus said. "We'll start moving rocks until we can inch our way out."

Before Vanora could take another step, two huge nets were flung over their heads. Vanora screamed. Her cries echoed off the stone walls. Angus struggled against the netting to no avail.

The rocks suddenly rolled away, and in the light of the glowing moss, Trows crawled around them like spiders, hissing and whispering. Some of them burst into laughter, leaping in circles, slapping each other on the back, while others remained silent, sneering and jabbing at them with long sticks.

"Oh my gosh, they're even worse than I pictured," Vanora said. "Look at those sloping foreheads and flat faces. And they stink, too!"

"Shh," Angus said. "They'll hear you!"

"So what! How do you know they understand what we say? They don't look intelligent to me. Look how pointy their ears are."

One of the Trows growled and shook its hairy fist at her.

Angus glared at Vanora. "What are you trying to do, make them kill us faster?"

"I'm not going to let them intimidate me!"

Angus tried to pull the netting off, but it only tangled tighter around them. He reached into his pocket, searching for a knife. He gritted his teeth. How stupid it was to travel so unprepared.

"Let us go—now!" Angus demanded.

The Trows ignored him and hitched a long pole into the netting, lifting him off the ground and carrying him like a pig on a spit.

Behind him, Vanora was screaming.

"Leave her alone!" Angus yelled. He tried to pull the netting apart, struggling harder than ever.

The Trows carrying him nearly toppled over. A ferocious-looking leader, bigger and broader than the rest, came to Angus' side. It pulled out a long whip and struck several blows before Angus held up his hands to ward off the painful blows and stopped struggling. The sting of the whip made his eyes water and only served to make Angus angrier and more determined than ever.

Behind him, Vanora fought with two fat Trows. They were trying to string her netting up onto a long pole, but she kept biting and kicking at them. Finally, the Trow with the whip came up beside her and raised the weapon high. It snapped in the air and cracked across Vanora's thigh. She cried out, clutching her wounded leg.

The other Trows seized the opportunity and strung the netting over the pole. They swiftly lifted her off the ground, ignoring her screams of protest. The Trow lifted the whip again.

"Don't you dare!" Angus snarled.

The leader turned and grinned at Angus, enjoying the torment.

Angus narrowed his eyes, refusing to back down.

The Trow waved the whip around as if to show off and finally attached it to a loop on the side of his belt. He grunted and pointed to the others to follow.

The captors sang songs as they marched, eerie, low songs that sounded like death chants. Angus glanced back at Vanora, who was tangled in the thick netting. Her face was red with rage. She tried to kick at them through the netting. Only two Trows carried her, while four had hold of Angus. He struggled as hard as he could, making sure it wasn't easy for them.

The journey seemed to take forever. Angus' back ached, but every time he moved inside the netting it threw the Trows off balance. He swung hard from side to side, trying to topple them over, but another Trow came beside him and stabbed him with a sharp stick.

"Where are you taking us?" Angus demanded. "Hey!"

The Trow with the whip raged forward and cracked the whip across Angus' back. Pain seared his flesh. Angus gritted his teeth. They could whip him all they wanted. He'd never give up. Not now.

The creatures continued onward, ignoring Angus every time he tried to communicate with them. Maybe the Trows couldn't talk or understand what he was saying. They didn't even turn their heads as he yelled in protest.

Vanora was twice as loud as Angus. She kicked and screamed with all her might. Occasionally, when a Trow got too close she would lash out and kick. They seemed to enjoy tormenting her more than Angus. With every cry, or kick, or scratch, they retaliated by snatching strands of her hair through the netting and pulling it hard. They laughed and poked at her until she screamed even louder.

They journeyed through one dark tunnel after another until they reached a wide expanse with a stone path that led to a massive bridge over a large body of flowing water. Carefully, the Trows treaded across the bridge, paying more attention to the water than to their captives. Angus peered down. What was it about water that made them so fearful? Was there something in it, or was it the water itself?

Two of the Trows stumbled and swung Angus over the high expanse. He stared down at the current, fifty feet below. Angus clamped his eyes shut, waiting for it to be over with. He hated heights more than anything. At least the water would break his fall, but if he became tangled in the netting he would certainly drown. And what about Vanora? He couldn't leave her with the Trows. But instead of letting him fall, they swung the netting back to safety, laughing and jeering at him.

The Trows paused to rest on the other side of the bridge, waiting for the others. As the other creatures were halfway across with Vanora, she lashed out with her foot, causing the fat Trow to pitch forward and nearly topple over the side of the bridge into the water. The creature whirled around and shook his fist at a skinny Trow, who stood directly behind him.

"Don't you shake your fist at me!" he growled.

So they *could* talk! And he could understand them, as well!

The Trow with the whip punched the skinny one in the face. Another jumped on his back, biting and pounding with its fists.

A fat one holding Angus let out a long growl. "Enough, you fools!"

The creatures scowled at each other. The skinny one stuck out a long, snake-like tongue at the fat one. "I'll get you later. Smash your head in with a rock while you sleep."

"Silence!" the head Trow yelled.

They had only walked a few feet when the skinny one pinched another Trow and then pointed at the fat one. Another fight broke out. Vanora took advantage of the opportunity, struggling to escape the netting.

One of the Trows carrying Angus dropped the pole. He ran at the fighting crowd and knocked them to the ground.

Angus scrambled to get free of the netting, but another Trow stood guard, painfully stabbing at him with every move Angus made. The pole carrier returned and hoisted Angus up in the netting again, continuing onward. Angus hated the way he couldn't touch the ground. How would he ever get free now? The Trows rounded a corner that led into a vast cavern. It was brightly lit with glowing moss.

The Trows swung Angus to the ground. He yanked the netting off himself, and before he could recover he was jerked upright and pushed forward. Vanora was dropped equally hard. She fought the netting off and was pushed to Angus' side. The Trows poked at them with their sticks, forcing the two toward a narrow path that led down a steep cliff.

Trow Towers was far bigger than he expected. Housed in a vast cavern, it was lit throughout by the same slimy fungus and oily torchlight as in the tunnel. The fungus grew alongside the paths that ribboned through the city. It covered every rooftop, filled flower boxes, and made up entire gardens.

It was a city of moss, stone and water. On the far side of the village, a wide river rushed over a tall cliff, creating a huge, underground waterfall. This river flowed through the center of the city, where numerous, oddly constructed bridges and tall fences crossed it.

"They don't like the water," Angus whispered to Vanora.

"Of course they don't. All stinky, vile creatures hate water." She scowled at the Trows. "In one of my father's books, it says the water will dissolve them. Water in its natural state is considered pure. It's part of their curse. They were forced down here because they were so evil. Now they must live surrounded by water. It's a punishment for them, I suppose. Plus, it helps keep them trapped."

"So, all we have to do is get them in the water, and that's it?" Angus whispered.

"I don't think it will be that easy." Vanora lowered her voice. "They'll know what you are up to, Angus. Trows are nasty creatures, but they aren't dumb."

"Did you see the way they beat up each other?"

"That's only natural for them. From what I've learned, Trows are taught to show absolutely no weakness from the moment they are born. If they show any positive emotions or do any actions other than evil, they are beaten, bullied, or even killed."

"Look!" Angus pointed to the center of the village. "It's Trow Towers." Four crumbling towers sprouted at odd angles from the structure's stone walls. Crooked bridges stretched from tower to tower. A pig's head with giant tusks was carved in the center of each of them.

The Trows pushed them forward into a maze of streets that seemed to wind this way and that, without any rhyme or reason. Perhaps the design was meant to disorientate their prey so that it couldn't escape. After a while, Angus realized that the place was almost totally free of any straight lines. It was like one huge, confusing maze. The buildings were crooked, as well, and some seemed to have no doors at all. They were more like cages or boxes than houses.

As they entered the heart of the city, Angus' gut tightened. Hundreds of Trows scurried about, scrambling madly like ants in the streets, swinging from the lampposts, leaping from roof to roof, and jeering and heckling the prisoners. Angus reached for Vanora's hand; if he could keep her close, maybe they could somehow escape. But one of the Trows stabbed his hand, almost piercing through the center of his palm.

"Ouch!" Angus reached out to grab the creature, wanting to take the stick and break it in half, but suddenly he was surrounded by Trows screaming and shouting.

They shoved Angus ahead, forcing him down a long, stone walkway that stretched from the village to the castle. Angus peered over his shoulder at Vanora, who, somehow, was close behind.

"What do they want with us?" Angus asked.

Vanora shrugged. "Hope they don't plan on eating us."

"Quiet!" the fat Trow shouted.

They crossed the moat and continued into a long courtyard, where they traveled through a second set of doors, through the castle, and into a giant throne room. Trows were lined up everywhere, hooting and screeching. Some of them were short and fat, with long, skinny tails, while others were tall and thin with wide drooling mouths.

Sitting on the throne was the ugliest creature Angus had ever seen. It was a very old Trow with small, glaring, pus-yellow eyes and a pointy nose dripping snot. The creature's hair was completely white; its knobby hands clutched a long staff for support. Beside the throne and throughout the room, urns of glowing fungus sprouted everywhere.

"Why have you invaded Trow Towers?" the Trow King asked.

"We didn't mean to trespass. We just got lost, and—"

"Liars! We know why you've come. We have spies, you know. Through the crevices and cracks we heard your meeting with the hobgoblins. We know you've come for the cat statue. How stupid do you think we are?"

"Pretty stupid, if you ask me," Vanora said.

The Trow King struck out with his stick, knocking Vanora hard across the face. Her glasses flew off, and when she went to retrieve them, the king stuck his foot over them.

"How bad do you want them, little girl-child?" the king sneered.

"Please! I can't see without them!"

Trows crept closer and closer, laughing and jeering. The king snatched up her glasses and tossed them into crowd.

"No!" Vanora cried.

"Give them back!" Angus shouted.

The trows laughed even harder. They danced around the king, tossing the spectacles to one another, pretending to drop them.

"Quit messing around!" the king growled. He waved his staff, and the Trows tossed the glasses around until they slid to the floor by Vanora's feet. She grabbed them, quickly wiped them off, and slipped them on.

The king narrowed his eyes at Angus. "You can have your statue. In fact, I have it right here." He held out a marble stone carved into a cat.

Angus reached for it. The stone figure sprang open, and something sharp jabbed into the palm of his hand. "Ouch!" he cried. A spiny creature jumped from Angus' hand to the ground and scurried away.

The king threw back his head and laughed. "Do you think I'm foolish enough to have the statue right here where you can steal it?"

"We don't steal!"

"But you'd do anything to get it, wouldn't you? Anything to save the old wizard, isn't that right?"

"What do you want from us?" Angus asked.

The king narrowed his eyes. "A bargain. A trade, of sorts." The king turned his attention to Vanora and licked his fat lips. Drool dripped from the corner of his mouth as he studied her closely. For a terrible second, Angus thought he wanted to trade the cat for Vanora, but instead, the king whipped his head back to Angus and pinned him with his horrible, yellow eyes. "We want you to release us from the spell the old wizard cursed us with—the one that keeps us trapped here. We want to return to the dark forests where we once lived, free to rob and to plunder."

"What do you want with me, then?" Angus exclaimed. "I'm not a magician. I can't break spells."

"Of course you can. You are the descendant of the king. And the king can break the spell."

"Angus, don't do it. There was a reason for Fane cursing them to this place," Vanora blurted out.

"Silence!" The king narrowed his eyes at Vanora and pointed a crusty finger. "One more sound, and I'll have your tongue cut out of your head and eat it for dinner."

Vanora's eyes went round; her skin paled.

The king leaned in her direction. He narrowed his eyes to mere slits. "Do you understand me? Not one word, or I'll slice it right out of your foolish head."

Vanora glared at him.

Angus' heart leapt. If Vanora was foolish enough to utter any sound, Angus knew the king would have her tongue.

"Okay!" Angus said. "Give me the statue first. Then I'll do it."

The king paused. "Why should I do that?"

"Because it's the only way I'll do it. And another thing." Angus balled up his fists. "I don't appreciate you threatening my friends." He took Vanora's hand. "Give me the statue."

The old Trow crinkled his eyes, and a scowl played on his lips. "Fair enough." He kicked at a Trow standing near. "Go get the statue, and give it to the boy king."

The Trow sneered at Angus and then scurried off.

The hall erupted in commotion. Trows screamed and laughed. Angus leaned close to Vanora and whispered into her ear. "We have to get to the water. If we can get into the water we can escape."

"Tell them you need the power of the water to help you, or make up something that sounds reasonable."

Angus thought for a moment. His mind raced; he had to come up with something quick.

The Trow returned with a dirty, brown, leather bag and

handed it to the king. The king held it for a moment, then tossed the bag to Angus.

Angus opened it with caution, and his heart leapt. Inside rested the cat statue. It was the size of a football, and pure white as if it were made of snow.

"Now, break the spell, boy, and be quick about it!" the king barked.

Several Trows surrounded him, pointed sticks raised. Angus held up a hand. "I'll do it. But I'll need the power of the water to help me."

The king scowled and shuffled closer. "What are you up to?"

"Nothing. It's just the way it works. As you must know, I'm part Selkie as well as king. I have to be near water for this to work." Angus frowned at the king. "Do you want me to do this, or not?"

The king thought for a moment. "All right, but the girl stays with us."

"No. She will stand beside me, or I won't do it."

Angus took Vanora's hand. Together they hurried out of the castle to the open grounds and up to the long bridge spanning high over the water. Trow guards followed close behind them. Angus looked down and swallowed hard. A wash of dizziness gripped him. He closed his eyes.

"It's okay, Angus—just don't look down," Vanora whispered.

He leaned in close. "I know, but the only way we're getting out of here is to jump in. Get ready."

Vanora stared into the milky flow and nodded.

Trows from all around slinked closer and closer.

Angus held the cat statue with both hands and dangled it over the water. Closing his eyes he pretended to mutter ancient words. All around, the Trows grew restless, whispering and hissing to one another. Angus opened his eyes and grabbed Vanora's hand. "Jump!"

Angus held tight to the statue as he fell, and he hit the water with a tremendous splash behind Vanora. He fought to rise to the surface, but it was like being cast into a boiling pot. The currents pulled at his shoes, tossing him around until he wasn't sure which way was up. He burst to the surface just in time to hear the King yell, "Traitors! Get them!"

A current whisked them away from the village. Behind them came great splashes. "I thought you said they didn't like water." Angus shot a glance behind him.

Several Trows were floating on scraps of wood. They paddled hard, gaining quickly on them.

"Swim harder!" Angus yelled.

Several of the creatures caught up to them. They struck out with their sticks, hitting Angus hard. He pulled a long stick away from a fat Trow and knocked it off its wooden boat. The creature screamed, gurgled, and melted into a thick glob before sinking into the deep. Angus climbed aboard and paddled hard to help Vanora, knocking more creatures into the water in the process. One by one, the creatures howled as they melted into blobs of fat and sank in the river. The waters suddenly boiled. Creatures rose from the depths, feasting on the remains of the fallen trows.

Vanora shivered and scrambled aboard her own chunk of wood, and they swiftly left the rest of the Trows behind.

Angus took out his map. It was soggy, but he could still read it. *The sea witch's cavern should be just ahead to your right. Keep a close lookout; you never know what you might run into.*

"I can only imagine," Vanora groaned. "At least we have the statue."

"Yes, and that is all that matters. Now we must get the sea witch to tell us how to keep it from getting stolen again."

The way grew murky as they traveled deeper into the cave. A mist seemed to form around them that sent chills up Angus' spine. The water stilled—almost as if time, itself, had been suspended. Seaweed glowed a strange green from the bottom of the water as they traveled. The temperature grew colder the farther they floated.

"Brrr, it's freezing in here." Vanora's teeth chattered.

"Look! There are lights up around the corner."

Torches flickered on the walls ahead. As they drew near, Angus could see they were really candles sticking into skulls fixed to the walls. Vanora ducked her head and just missed a glob of spider webs. "Yuck! What's with all the spiders down here?"

"That's not the worst of it." Angus swallowed hard. "Did you see the fish heads? They're floating everywhere in the water."

"Let's hope she isn't as creepy as her surroundings, or we're in trouble."

They came to a stone ledge with a large, wooden door. On the front were the words *Enter only if you dare.*

They climbed from their wooden boats onto the ledge. Angus picked up a metal knocker shaped like a clamshell and knocked twice. The door creaked open. They entered into a shadowy cave, where only candles lit the way. Dried seaweed and netting blanketed the floor, and shells and Japanese glass floats hung on the walls. Hundreds of glass bottles in all shapes and sizes hung, suspended by ropes, from the ceiling. Angus tried to make out what was in them. Some looked to contain leathery creatures—petrified frogs and snakes—while others contained herbs and slimy concoctions.

"What do you think all the bottles are for?" Angus whispered.

"The animals are probably for casting evil spells. The herbs must be seasoning for cooking children."

"Children!"

"You know, like Hansel and Gretel."

Angus shuddered. "Let's hope not. You really should get some help for that imagination of yours."

"Hey, at least I'm aware of the dangers of a place like this. Don't you think it's better to be prepared?"

"Who dares to enter my home?" a creaky voice spoke from the darkness.

Angus and Vanora froze.

"We do, ma'am. My name is Angus MacBain, and I'm here with my friend, Vanora. We need to speak with you… please," Angus said.

Vanora grasped Angus' hand. "This place smells like dead fish," she whispered.

"Quiet! She might hear you."

The voice came again. "What is it you seek?"

"We need your help. We have an object that was taken from the island of Iona. It is a special statue that allows my advisor, Fane Vargovic, to travel between worlds. He is trapped now, and—"

"I know of your plight. You are part of the sea, are you not, Young King?"

"Yes, my mother—"

"Stop explaining! Come forward. But only you—not the human girl."

Angus looked at Vanora.

She dropped his hand. "Be careful, Angus."

He walked forward into another part of the cave; a round table dominated the center of a small room.

"Place your object on the table."

Angus took the cat from the bag and held it to his chest for a moment. Could he trust the sea witch? What if she took it for herself?

"Put it down. I have no reason to covet such a thing."

Could she read his mind? "I'm sorry, it's just that—"

"Put it down! And be careful that you do not wake the dead." The woman's voice seemed to echo across the cave.

As Angus approached the table, he spotted barrels—no doubt lost from ships—lining the wall. Skeletal hands and the tops of skulls and thighbones protruded from them. Angus stopped short. "What are those things?"

"Those are people who have come to challenge me. Those who have lost their lives at sea because they lacked respect for the power of the ocean."

Angus set the statue carefully on the table. Something in one of the barrels moved, and Angus jumped backward.

The sea witch emerged from the shadows. At first, she appeared to be a rotting pile of rags, but then Angus made out it was a dress, and she wore a thin black veil to cover her entire head. She moved as if floating above the floor and snatched the statue in clawed hands. Angus wanted to take it back, but the creature was so foul and terrifying that Angus kept his distance. But in the faint candlelight she looked familiar. His heart raced. Could it be? Prudence?"

"It is my sister's likeness you see—is it not, Young King? Have no fear. I have no ties to her; she serves the Dark One." The witch's voice lowered into a deep, dark tone. "There is no other I despise more than Dragomir for his attacks upon those that dwell in the sea." The sea witch paused. "I will cast a spell over this statue, but on one condition… you must promise to follow my instructions precisely. Is that agreeable?"

Angus nodded. "What do I need to do?"

"You will place the statue in its spot only when there is no moon visible. Moonlight in a graveyard will render the spell useless. You must keep it covered until you place it in its rightful spot. Do you understand?"

Angus nodded.

"There is one more thing you must do. You must take a handful of dirt from a loved one's grave and dig a trench around the headstone where the cat statue will be placed. Sprinkle the dirt in a complete circle around the stone, then cover it up and press it down firmly. This will add the extra protection it will need to remain fixed in place. Any evil entity that dares take the stone will suffer a 'grave' fate if they so much as touch it."

The witch turned her back, rubbing her hands over the object and muttering words Angus could not understand. She placed it in a leather sack and handed it back to Angus. Going to a dark corner of the room, she returned with a large brown candle and placed it on the table alongside a yellowed piece of paper, a pen, and a quill.

She handed Angus the quill and pointed to the parchment with a long, black fingernail. "Write your name here."

Angus studied the paper; it looked very old. There was nothing written on it. When he leaned forward to write his name, it moved.

"Never mind that," the witch said. "Sign, and it will grant you protection while you set the stone."

Angus signed, and the sea witch quickly grabbed the parchment, spun it towards herself, and drew a circle around Angus' signature. She held her hands over the paper. "Goddess of the sea, keeper of the waters free, guide and guard the young king. May this statue's curse to *him* no harm bring. Lady of Wave and Foam, heed this spellwork poem." The sea witch paused, inhaled a rattling breath, then turned to Angus. "Go now. May the power of the moon and tides be with you."

"I have another question," Angus said. "Your sister put a spell on my friend's dad. It's like he's frozen, and—"

"There is nothing more I can tell you. It could have been any number of conjurings. I cannot be of help in that matter."

"All right, thank you. For the help with the statue."

The sea witch nodded, lowered her head, and seemed to float backward, blending into the dark wall.

Angus hurried from the room and grabbed Vanora's hand. "Come on." This place gives me the creeps." They fled the cavern.

"Did you get her to put a spell on the statue?"

"I did. Hopefully it will work and get this whole mess resolved. I also told her about your dad."

"What did she say?"

Angus shook his head. "She couldn't help us. She said it could be any number of spells or whatever."

"That sucks."

"I know. I'm really sorry. But we're going to find a way. Just don't give up, okay?"

Vanora nodded. "I won't. Not ever."

"Good. We better get going."

Angus held Vanora's scrap of wood so that she could climb on. After she was safely seated, he scrambled onto his own, and they paddled away.

"I hate the way this water feels." Vanora shivered. "It's so slimy."

"You're lucky you didn't see what else she had in there." Angus scowled. "Everything was so gross. I can't wait to get out into the open again." He reached into his pocket and withdrew the map. He studied it for a few moments.

"Well, what does it say?"

"It says if we keep going the direction we're heading now, it will lead us to open water and then home."

"Good, I can't wait."

Vanora and Angus rowed deeper into the dark.

They floated into a series of caverns, each one darker than the last. Beneath them, creatures slithered and writhed in the murky waters, weaving in and out of bones and giant ribcages with flesh still clinging to them.

"Something touched my foot!" Vanora yanked her feet up onto the log.

"Shh." Angus pointed to one of the huge, snakelike creatures that swirled underneath them. It swam away in a big loop, then turned and slithered on top of the water in Vanora's direction.

"Angus, help!"

The monster struck her log with such force that Vanora flew into the air before splashing into the water backwards. She burst to the surface and screamed as the creature reared its massive head high out of the water. It looked like a giant eel with a spiny back and close-set eyes. It made a move to lunge at her, when Angus screamed, "Vanora!"

The giant eel shifted its attention to Angus, then turned and thrust itself at Vanora again. It was gone in an instant, with Vanora flailing and screaming in its jaws.

"Vanora!" Several painful seconds passed. Angus leaned over the water, his heart in his throat. The creature suddenly burst to the surfaced with Vanora dangling like an overcooked noodle in its gaping mouth.

For a moment, Angus thought she was dead, impaled on the creature's massive teeth, but then she struggled, trying to free herself from between the creature's fangs.

"Let me go!" Vanora screamed. She knotted her fist and beat it between the eyes. The creature dove under the water again.

Angus sucked in his breath—the serpent was trying to drown her so it could eat her! He lept off his log. In the murky water, he saw the creature dive deeper and deeper with Vanora in its jaws. Angus dove too, kicking hard. He grabbed the tip of its tail, pulled himself closer, and bit down with all his might. The creature kept going, descending into the murky unknown.

Just when Angus thought his lungs would burst, they entered a narrow expanse clogged with the bones of warriors clad in rusting armor. Angus snatched a sword from a skeletal hand and slashed at the creature with one hand while he held tight to its tail with the other. Blood spilled from the monster's side.

The creature flung Vanora free and turned to snap long fangs at Angus. Angus braced himself and swung onto the creature's back. The beast rose to the surface, clacking its immense jaws in fury. Strings of thick ooze glistened from its fangs. It bit at the dense air, its immense body slithering in tight circles all the while. The frantic beast battered itself against the cavern wall, trying to knock Angus loose. Angus raised the sword to stab at the creature, but the beast moved and twisted so fast it was all Angus could do to hold on.

The beast rose up hard, striking the ceiling with its neck. The impact unleashed an avalanche of stalactites. One of them missed Angus by inches and stabbed into the creature's spine. The sea monster threw itself into a fury of twisting and writhing, snapping blindly in every direction. Its body rolled into tight coils as its colossal head whipped back and forth.

Angus flew from the creature's back, hit the rock wall, and slid into the frothy water. Everything went black. Then, slowly, his vision returned. The blow to his head made his legs and arms too heavy to move. His shattered mind raced. If only he had the strength to paddle his arms, kick his legs, pull his head above water, and survive. Water slid down his throat and filled his inflamed lungs, drowning out the sounds of Vanora's panicked screams. Angus released the tightness in his chest and closed his eyes as darkness swallowed all.

11

The Journey Home

A symphony of sounds washed over Angus as he sank into the darkest depths, cradled in the soft, salty water. He opened his eyes to a bright light in the center of an underwater whirlpool. The light changed, becoming more solid. Was this the way to heaven? Would his mother know that he had died?

A golden merman carrying a long trident burst through the tunnel. He swam directly at Angus, approaching so rapidly Angus thought they might collide. Angus squinted; he wasn't positive the merman was real until he took hold of Angus' arms and raced toward the surface. When they exploded from the water, Angus coughed water from his lungs, gasping for breath.

"We're here to help you, Young King," the merman said.

"What about my friend? I lost her, and…"

The merman smiled. "No worries; she is waiting in a boat we have provided for you."

A surge of relief washed over Angus. "Thank you. I was afraid that...."

"There is no need for concern, and there is no need to thank me. For now, all is well."

The merman guided him over the waves and through the choppy water to a long, glass canoe. Angus was surprised to see the vessel being pulled by two giant sea turtles. They had thick, green shells with gold and silver adorning the sides. On each foot was a set of massive flippers. They had long, skinny necks, which they used to gawk at Angus. The turtles didn't appear happy to see him; in fact, it looked as if they were scowling at him.

Vanora peered over the side. "Oh, Angus. I'm so glad you're okay. I was scared stiff." The merman hoisted Angus up so he could climb into the boat. Vanora leaned over to help.

The turtles turned and snapped. "Watch out!" Vanora said. "They're really crabby, and they like to bite! One nearly took my finger off."

Angus flopped into the boat and scrambled to get upright. He slid onto the seat beside Vanora. The turtles continued to glare at him.

The merman slipped aboard with ease. To Angus' amazement, his fins had transformed into long, lean legs. The merman shot the turtles an angry glance. "My apologies for their behavior. We didn't have much choice in getting help on such short notice." The merman sighed. "These turtles can be quite inhospitable and have terrible memories."

Vanora wrapped her arms around Angus' neck. "Never mind the turtles, I'm just so happy to see you. I thought that horrible creature had killed you!"

"Thanks. To be honest, I was pretty worried myself." Angus turned his attention to the merman. "How did you know I was in trouble?"

"Your mother. She sent a distress signal. Asked for help from anyone nearby. You're lucky I heard her call—she's many nautical miles away from here, plus, she fades in and out of a deep and restful sleep. She could never have fully awoken and gotten to you in time."

"How did she know I was in trouble?"

"The water tells her everything," the merman said. "She is greatly saddened to hear the news of Fane Vargovic. She also understands why you are on this quest and not in school."

"Sad news? You mean he's…"

The merman shook his head. "No, that is not what I meant. He lives still, but just barely. A prisoner, of sorts. Much like your mother, the poor soul."

"My mother? What do you mean?"

"Fane is trapped between two worlds," the merman said. "A lot like your mother is. She struggles to exist in two totally different lives—one in a magical realm and another in the world of mankind. This is no easy task."

"I know, and it's hard for me too. I never know if she's okay. I hate the fact that I can't speak to her. I don't even know where she goes when she disappears into the sea."

"She goes to the great kelp forest. It is a place far removed from here, a special area where Selkies go to rest. The seal people rejuvenate in the velvety-smooth kelp, lithe and loving, and they are fed by the lush plant, enriched by the nutrients it holds."

"It sounds like such a peaceful place," Vanora said.

"It truly is. The kelp forests are the most beautiful of all." The creature sighed. "But even in such a place of beauty, your mother is constantly trapped between two parallels. She feels the worry of motherhood when she is away and can never truly rest, as most do." The merman paused. "You have to understand that even though your mother has a happy life on land, there will always be a part of her that will yearn for the sea, and, at times, she will be disconnected from the worries and joy of humanity."

The merman grabbed hold of long, silver reins attached to the turtles and snapped them on the hard shells. The turtles rose half out of the water and lunged forward, taking off at top speed through the dark cavern.

Angus lifted his head. "Where is Fane?"

"He is trapped in limbo between Ceòban and this world, and he is fading quickly. I shudder to think what would have happened if we had been just a few minutes longer. These waters are filled with many dangerous beasts."

Angus' heart twisted. "Is he going to be okay?"

The merman nodded. "There is still time, but you must make haste. You must return the statue to Iona as soon as possible." He lowered his voice. "You must take great care—word has already gotten out that you escaped the Trows with the statue. The dark forces are regrouping."

"Will you take us to Iona?"

"No, I am afraid I cannot. We do not journey that close to the shores of mankind. But have no worries; the turtles will take you. As soon as your feet hit the shore, hurry as fast as you can to place the stone where the original once sat. It is critical to Fane's survival that you do not waste a single second. "

"When will we see him again?" Vanora asked.

The merman slowly shook his head. "We do not know. It's never a good thing to tarry between worlds, and, sadly, he has been stuck there quite a long time. It's a good thing you heard him when he reached out to you. Now, hold on with all your might."

The boat took off like lightning. They sped through several caves so fast the walls and water blurred together. Finally, they came to a solid-rock wall.

"Goodbye, and good luck to you," the merman said, before jumping off the boat. The boat sped up, heading straight toward the rock wall. Angus' heart leapt into his throat.

"Where did he go?" Vanora shouted.

Angus shook his head. "I don't know! But it looks like we're going to crash!"

"Look out!" Vanora exclaimed.

Angus pulled Vanora to him and clamped his eyes shut, waiting for the terrible collision. But the boat passed through the stone and into open water without a scratch—as if there had never been a wall at all. The vessel slowed and then came to a halt just outside Fingal's Cave.

"Thank goodness." Vanora clutched her chest. "That was a bit too close for my taste."

Angus fought to catch his breath. "Me too." He surveyed his surroundings. The boat floated in the choppy waters. "Looks like we're back where we started. Let's get out of here before Ferock causes trouble. "

Evening was upon them. Black clouds loomed

overhead, almost concealing part of a full moon.

"At least we'll have some light yet," Vanora said.

Angus grabbed the reins. He had no idea how to steer turtles. He clutched the straps and flicked them hard. The turtles floated in the water, ignoring him.

"What am I doing wrong?"

Vanora shrugged. "I don't know. Try again—this time with more confidence."

Angus snapped the reins. But again, nothing happened. The turtles floated in the water.

"Wait a second," Vanora said.

"What?"

"Listen. I hear soft voices."

Angus listened. Sure enough, he could make out whispering. He leaned forward and saw the turtles were talking to one another.

"Why should we take them anywhere? We're magic turtles, not workhorses."

"I hear you, Amos, and they could have picked someone else for this. You know I don't like being out in the open sea."

"Hey!" Angus interrupted.

The turtles looked over their shells at him. "What do you want?"

"I'd like to go, if it isn't too much trouble to you." Heat rose under his shirt collar. "I need to get back to Iona as quickly as possible. Lives are at stake!"

"Well, why didn't you say so?" the turtle on the left said. It turned to the turtle on the right. "No one told me it was an emergency. Did they tell you, Stanley?"

The turtle shook its head. "No one told me."

"Please, can we just go now?"

"All right, but just so you know, we didn't sign on for this. We're turtles. We're not cut out for this sort of thing."

"Whatever, just get going." Angus snapped the reins, and with a grumble, the turtles reared back and charged ahead. The boat spun in a large circle and headed out to sea.

"Were going in the wrong direction!" Vanora yelled.

Angus pulled back on the reins, but the turtles kept going.

"Hey!" he yelled, but the turtles only traveled faster. "I think they're confused! I can't stop them."

"Relax your grip on the reins! They think you want to go faster!"

Angus let loose on the reins, and the turtles slowed. "Hey, it's this way," he yelled.

"What way?" the turtles called in unison.

"North, to the island, to Iona. Just like I told you a second ago!"

"Oh, that's right. I completely forgot," the turtle on the left said.

"Sheesh, so much fuss over nothing. You'll be lucky if you don't wear us out," the other turtle snorted.

The creatures turned and headed for the island, but suddenly they stopped.

Vanora grabbed Angus' arm. "Why are they stopping? We have to hurry!"

"Hey!" Angus yelled. "What's going on?"

The turtles remained frozen, and then they suddenly looked at one another, eyes wide in fear. Without notice, they whirled around, chomped the reins in half, dove into the depths, and disappeared, leaving Angus and Vanora stranded.

"Where are you going?" Angus called after them.

A dark mist clouded around them. A bell rang three times. Ghostly sails flapped as the prow of a great ship broke through the mist in the distance.

Vanora gasped. Angus turned to look into her panic-stricken face. "Oh my gosh! It's the Black Mary! What are we going to do, Angus?"

"Don't freak out. Just stay calm."

"Stay calm? Are you kidding me?"

"Shh!" Angus whispered. "Be as quiet as you can."

"What good will that do?"

"Quick—look for some oars!"

"There!" Vanora pointed to two wooden oars resting under Angus' feet.

The boat drew closer, froth churning off its massive bow as it plowed up and down through the swells. The timbers let out a terrible groan from their eternal labor at sea. The ship's bell rang three times again.

Vanora peered into the boiling water. "Did you hear that? How creepy!"

Angus nodded as he snapped the oars into the oarlocks on each side of the boat.

"I still can't believe those stupid turtles left us to die!"

"Well, what do you expect from angry sea turtles? It wasn't as if they were friendly or even sane."

The ship drew closer. A horrible stench of death filled the air. Pirates lined the deck with long cutlasses hanging at their sides.

Vanora sucked in a breath. "What are we going to do?"

"Is there anything we can offer them? Maybe we can trade them something."

"That's not what they want, Angus. They aren't like regular pirates. They collect other things... souls to man the ship and work the decks."

Angus swallowed hard. "You'd think they have enough crewmembers by now. I mean, after all the centuries they've been wandering the sea."

"Yes, but pirates are greedy—they can never have enough."

The ship charged full speed at them.

"Faster, Angus! They're coming for us!"

Angus pulled hard on the oars. "I'll never be able to outrow them!"

They entered a large fog bank.

"You're right, we can't outrun them," Vanora said.

"What if they crash into us?"

"What other choice do we have?" Vanora said.

The ship sliced through the water. Seawater slid off the massive bow as it rose up, high into the air and crashed down again through the monstrous, rolling swells. Vicious winds howled at her sails, tainting the air with more of her foul smell. A terrible, morbid groan sounded as the timbers continued to complain. Oil lamps swung back and forth on deck, creating an eerie reflection against the fog. The vessel's rigging glowed grey and black, and its tattered flag beat like a broken wing against the mast. The ship's wheel on the quarterdeck turned in mad circles, spinning out of control without a hand to control and navigate the waters.

Angus pulled the agate eyeglass from his pocket. A

ghostly crew, swords drawn, pointed at them. The captain, who looked more a part of the sea than human, stood behind the wheel, eyes blazing. His tangled, fire-coral beard crawled with crabs and sea urchins, and his hair waved in the wind like angry, venomous snakes.

"It's not slowing down, Angus! It's coming right for us!"

"We have to get out of here!" Angus dropped the eyeglass into his pocket and grabbed the oars. He pulled hard on them, but it was no use; the ship was coming at them too fast.

"Jump!" Vanora yelled.

Angus tucked the statue under his arm and dove into the sea, swimming as hard and as fast as he could. The pirates jumped in after them. Once under the water, the men changed from pirates into hideous sea creatures—half-man, half-shark, with fishy eyes and jagged teeth in their skull-like faces. Angus struggled to swim with the cat tucked under one arm. A few feet to the left, one of the pirates snatched at Vanora's legs.

Angus swam as fast as he could to reach her, but the pirate was already heading to the surface. Determined to reach her, Angus kept swimming. He gripped her arm and tried to pull her away, but he was suddenly surrounded by pirate-beasts. They grabbed at him, trying to drag him to the surface, but Angus fought hard, kicking and hitting. He swung at one of the men, a pirate who'd bared his teeth at Angus, trying to bite him. The man's teeth grazed Angus' skin, and the cat slipped out of his hand. Angus turned to grab it, but it was sinking fast as more pirates surrounded him.

Angus burst free and dove after it, barely grabbing the statue before it was lost in the depths forever. Pirates at his heels grabbed at his legs and arms. He raced to the surface, when suddenly, one of the pirates snatched him and pulled him back.

Out of nowhere swam a bale of giant turtles, and the two that had pulled the canoe were leading the group. Angus grabbed onto the back of one of them, and it took him to the surface. Angus gasped for air. Clinging the back of the turtle, he looked frantically around for Vanora. He spotted her being pulled by a pirate toward the ship.

Before Angus could rescue Vanora, one of the turtles rose from the depths. It bit the pirate in the back of the neck and pulled it down into the depths, freeing Vanora.

"We can handle the rest of them," one of the turtles said. "Hang on, and we will take you and the girl to shore."

"Thank you!" Angus said.

Vanora came to his side riding on the back of the other turtle. "Yes, thank you! We thought you deserted us."

"Oh, we wouldn't have done that. When we saw the ship, we went for help. We can't swim as fast in open water when evil is draining our power." The turtle shook its head. "You humans are always getting yourselves into trouble."

"I'm sure glad you helped! Thanks again."

"It's not like we really wanted to. Hush up, and hold on tight."

The turtles took off with Vanora and Angus on their backs. The bitter, autumn air chilled Angus to the bone, whipping at his face until his cheeks burned. "Are you okay?" Angus yelled.

"Yes," Vanora yelled back. "Just freezing cold!"

"Keep your head down. We'll be to the island soon."

Vanora nodded and tucked her head down, holding on to the turtle's shell and bracing against the wind.

The gentle shores of Iona came into view. "We're almost there!" Angus said. "Just a few more minutes. Hang on!"

Near the shoreline, the turtles slowed to a stop, treading water. "This is as far as we go, I'm afraid," Angus' turtle said.

Angus and Vanora slid into the water.

"Thank you so much," Vanora said to her turtle.

"Yes, thank you." Angus said. "If not for you and your friends, we never would have made it home safe."

"You're welcome," Angus' turtle said. "All of us must work together to fight Lord Dragomir's evil."

The other turtle turned around and headed out to sea. "Better get back to our friends," it called over its shell. "I'm sure they can handle those pirates on their own, but you never know. Good luck to you." It dove into the water and disappeared.

The other turtle followed, kicking up water with its hind legs.

Angus and Vanora waded onto shore. Wet sand sucked at their feet while the bitter wind sent chills into their bones. They hurried toward the cemetery. "Come on, we gotta get this cat in place and then go check on my dad!"

Angus carried the sack with the cat statue under his arm and into the cemetery. He quickly traveled to the headstone with a chunk missing on top, where the other cat had once been. Angus paused and then peered up at the night sky.

"What in the world are you waiting for?" Vanora asked. "Hurry and put it in place so I can get to my dad."

"I know, I want to hurry but the sea witch said to wait until the moon was covered over with clouds or the spell would be useless."

Vanora wrinkled her nose and stared at the night sky. "Looks like there are some storm clouds to the east."

Something blustered past Angus' ear. "Did you feel that?" he asked.

"No, but I heard it. Sounded like wings. Could be a bat or…"

From somewhere in the haze, a large flock of crows emerged, zooming straight at them. The crow in the lead wore a large patch over its eye."

"It's Cudweed!" Vanora yelled. "And he's brought an army with him!"

Cudweed dove down on them. Vanora ducked. Cudweed missed her by inches. He swerved in flight and rose to dive again. He was joined by others—six, seven, a dozen—all changing shape and growing larger in size, hissing, with long, pink tongues flicking in and out.

Angus covered his head with his arms and tried to reach for Vanora, but the birds kept coming, filling the cemetery with the sounds of shrieking and beating wings. Blood ran down Angus' hands, wrists, and neck. Their sharp beaks tore at his arms, trying to get at his face. If only he could keep them away from his eyes. Nothing else mattered.

The crows clung to Angus' shoulders, ripping at his hair and clothes, diving en masse at his head. With each swoop, with each attack, they grew stronger, bolder, and angrier.

Angus knocked several to the ground, while others folded their wings and dove for his face. He grabbed some of the birds mid-flight, slamming them into the cemetery rock wall, where they fell to the grass, twitching. Others launched into the air for another attack.

Vanora picked up several rocks and flung them at the crows. The birds turned their attention from Angus, hovered for a moment, and then descended on Vanora. They ripped at her clothes and beat her back with their nasty, black wings. Vanora dropped to her stomach and covered her head. A rush of birds hovered over her motionless body, sitting on her and pulling at her hair.

Angus rushed to her side, kicked at the birds, and flapped his hands to drive them away. Cudweed flew up behind Angus, snatched the bag with the cat statue from his hand, and launched into the air. The birds left Vanora, following Cudweed.

"Quick, Angus! Do something!" Vanora screamed.

He grabbed a chunk of broken marble from one of the headstones and pitched it into the air. The rock hit Cudweed's foot, and the sack fell toward the ground. The other crows chased after it. Angus ran hard and tackled the sack. He rolled onto his back, pulled out the eyeglass and aimed the light at the birds. One by one, they disintegrated into ash. All except Cudweed, who disappeared into the horizon with his injured foot tucked beneath him.

Dark clouds swallowed the moon.

"The moon's behind the clouds!" Vanora yelled. "Hurry,

before something else tries to stop us!"

Angus pulled the statue out of the sack. He rushed to the grave and was about to place the statue to rest on top of the headstone when Cudweed dove from the sky. Angus ducked and scrambled to place the stone once again. Cudweed shrieked as he ran into a silver light beam. The light circled the statue, affixing the cat to the top of the stone. The bird flopped to the ground with such force that Angus expected Cudweed to be dead for sure. But the creature rose from the dirt, launched itself into the air again, and disappeared.

"We did it, Angus!" Vanora exclaimed.

"Not yet; I still have one more thing to do." Angus turned and strode to the edge of the cemetery. He found his grandfather's grave and knelt, emotions spilling over. He hadn't visited here since the old man's death. Scooping dirt from the top of the grave, he filled the sack that once contained the statue.

Angus dug a trench around the headstone where the cat statue was placed. He sprinkled his grandfather's dirt in a complete circle around the stone, then covered it and pressed it down with his palms. All at once, the ground became more solid. Then it hardened even more, transforming into solid, granite stone.

"Looks like the statue is safe. If anyone tries to touch it or remove it with evil intentions, they will be cursed, or worse… I'm not sure what kind of spell the old sea witch put on it."

"Good," Vanora said. "Let's get to my house."

They hurried down the path to her cottage. No light shone through the windows. No sign of movement.

Angus' heart fell.

As they stepped inside, Vanora rushed to the chair where her dad sat. She spun the chair around. There sat Mr. Pegenstecher, staring straight ahead. Although his body was visible, he was still frozen. What Angus found most shocking was that Mr. Pegenstecher's legs were green and fuzzy. It appeared they were turning into seaweed.

"We've got to get this spell off him, and fast—he's transforming into a sea creature!" Vanora exclaimed. "Probably a side effect of being cursed by a sea hag."

Angus swallowed hard. "Is he okay? I mean, is he still…"

Vanora grabbed her dad's wrist to check his pulse, and nodded. "He's still alive, but we need to get him awake. What can we do?"

Angus knotted his hands into fists. "I wish I had the answers, but I don't know. It's so frustrating."

A familiar voice broke into the room. "What is all the commotion about?"

Fane stood in the doorway. Angus and Vanora rushed to him. He looked tired and more gray, but very much alive.

"We need your help! Prudence put a curse on Vanora's dad. He's frozen. He's been this way since we left the island to find the cat statue."

Fane's eyes snapped open wide. "Take me to him—quickly."

Vanora grabbed Fane's hand and hurried him into the living room where he knelt at Mr. Pegenstecher's side. He spent a moment examining the man then stood up, his face filled with worry lines. "I'm sorry, but there is nothing I can do for him."

"Nothing you can do?" Angus said. "But you're a wizard! What do you mean?"

Fane headed outside. "There are things I cannot fix. Sadly, this is one of them. He will remain frozen until the spell wears off. Sometimes it takes longer than the human body can withstand."

Vanora's eyes filled with tears. "There *must* be a way to wake him. There *has* to be!"

Fane hugged Vanora. "Time will tell. Get some warm blankets and start a fire. Keep him as comfortable as possible."

They returned inside and started a roaring fire. Fane lit his pipe and studied Mr. Pegenstecher. He withdrew his pipe from his lips and pointed it at Vanora's dad. "There's something we're missing. Something evil is at play here."

Angus exchanged worried glances with Vanora.

"He should have awakened when you placed the statue in its proper place." Fane smoothed a hand over his beard. He cast his gaze around the room. "Something wicked has gotten a firm foothold here. It has to be a hag's bag, a relic, or some other magical trinket. It's something that lingers long after the spell caster is gone. Angus, use your eyeglass and tell me what you see."

Angus peered through the eyeglass. He saw Prudence once again, leaning over Mr. Pegenstecher. It was like a movie that had picked up where he last left it. She turned, grinning, and slinked out the doorway. Angus was just about to lower the eyeglass when Prudence scuttled back into the room, a small leather bag clutched in her hand.

She hurried to where Vanora's dad sat and tucked the bag into his shirt pocket.

Angus nearly dropped the eyeglass. "It's in his shirt pocket!"

Fane reached inside Mr. Pegenstecher's pocket and pulled the bag free. He wasted no time tossing the contents into the fire. A piercing scream sounded, and out of the flames flew a tiny sea hag riding a seahorse. As she buzzed close to Angus' face, he could see she was ugly, with a pointy chin and nose. She traveled faster and faster in a tight circle, screaming at the top of her tiny lungs. Like an angry insect, she dove first at Angus' head, then swooped to take a shot at Vanora, who ducked out of the way just in time.

Fane picked up a large fly swatter and slapped the hag out of the air in mid-flight. The seahorse buzzed away and out an open window. Angus bent to pick up the fallen creature and fling her into the fire, when Fane lurched forward to stop him. "Don't touch it! She'll give you a terrible case of blisters."

Vanora scowled. "What a horrible creature! Just look at those sharp claws and teeth!"

Angus knelt on the floor to study the fallen creature. The tiny sea hag had big, black eyes with no eyelids. Her skin was a crusted brown, and her lips were curled back, exposing needle-like teeth. She twitched furiously, clawing at the ground, struggling to get up.

Fane looked at Vanora. "Quick, get a cup of water and bring it here."

Vanora headed for the kitchen. "Make sure it's cold," Fane called after her.

She returned quickly with the water.

"Stand back!" Fane yelled. He doused the creature.

It let out a gruesome shriek before twisting and simmering into the floor.

"Gross! It stinks!" Angus waved his hand in front of his nose. "Ugh, I didn't know something so small could stink so bad."

Vanora's dad suddenly stretched and yawned. "Wow, I must have really been out."

Vanora ran to her father's side and threw her arms around his neck. "Dad! I'm so glad you're okay."

Mr. Pegenstecher blinked. "Why wouldn't I be? A good nap never hurt anyone." He spotted Fane and rose to his feet. "I'm sorry, I didn't know we had company."

Fane extended his hand. "Fane Vargovic. Nice to meet you, sir. You have quite a remarkable daughter; she's told me a lot about you."

Mr. Pegenstecher smiled. "And I've heard many good things about you from Angus. Pleasure to finally meet you, sir. I have many questions to ask."

"Yes, but I'm afraid it will all have to wait." Fane glanced at his wristwatch. "We've got a ferry to catch. I must bid farewell."

Angus felt a sharp pain in his chest. He wanted to beg Fane to stay with him on Iona instead of being forced to leave for school in Scotland, but the weary expression in Fane's eyes told him the old man needed to return home to rest. Maybe school wouldn't be so bad after all. He'd had enough adventure for one summer.

"Are you all right, Angus?" Fane asked.

Angus nodded.

"I'm proud of how you've handled things."

"Thanks. I know I should be happy that everything turned out okay; I just wish things didn't have to change so much. I mean, I had just gotten to know my mother again when she had to leave. And now I'll be going to a strange school in some place I've never been before. I can never count on anything. It's all so confusing."

"Life is filled with challenges, Angus, especially for one with a heritage such as yours. If life were easy, it would hardly be worth living. Would it?"

Angus lowered his head, and Fane placed a hand on his shoulder. "As much as you despise the ocean for taking your mother away from you, why not try listening to what it is trying to tell you? After all, part of you belongs to the sea as well as the land."

Angus shot Fane a curious look.

The old man released a weary sigh. "The cycle of the tides are a profound lesson in the inevitable changing of all things. They teach us that there is an ebb and flow to natural cycles, and that we must flow with them. I know this isn't easy for you, Angus, but in time I think you will come to realize that not all change is bad. Think of all you have gained instead of lost."

Angus nodded. He knew the old man was right. In the past few months, he had found his lost mother, gained the friendship of Vanora and Fane, and learned of a heritage he didn't know he had. But most of all, he had learned to believe in himself.

Angus packed his bags and locked the stone cottage he and his mother had shared for the summer. He stood on the porch and gazed out to the restless sea. With each cresting wave, he longed to see his mother. To tell her goodbye just once more before leaving for school—but sadly, that wasn't meant to be.

He closed his eyes and imagined his mother, with her beautiful, dark hair and eyes, resting in a palace made of seashells, surrounded by dancing gardens of kelp. He saw her swimming through forests of lush sea trees, dressed in her sealskin, with fur as silky and fine as an ocean wave.

Footsteps took him from his daydream. Vanora stood in front of him, smiling, with her hand out. "Ready to go?"

Angus nodded. "Ready as I'll ever be, I guess."

A wide grin spread across her face. "There's been a change in plans."

"Why? What's happening?"

Vanora clapped her hands. "It's the most exciting thing!"

"What?"

"Fane and my father have arranged for us to go to school in Ceòban." Vanora jumped up and down. "What do you think?"

Before Angus could take it all in, Vanora said, "Won't that just be the most amazing thing ever? Can you imagine all the cool things we will learn?"

Angus stared at Vanora. He could hardly believe what she was saying. "Are you sure?"

Vanora nodded. "You want to know the coolest part of all?"

"What?"

"My father will be going with us! Fane is going to teach him about the island and all about the creatures that live there. My father is so excited. It's like a dream come true. He's been wanting an opportunity like this his whole life."

"I'm happy for him, but why would Fane do that? I thought he didn't want humans to know."

"He wants someone he can trust to record it all, just in case… you know, something happens to him. He really had a close call last time."

Angus frowned. "I know it was, but I won't let anything happen to Fane. Not if I can help it."

"I know you love him, Angus, and you want to protect him. We all do, but it's still a good idea to have things recorded, just in case… in case, someday, Fane isn't here to help you."

Angus lowered his head. He hated the idea of losing another person close to him. "I guess you're right."

"Can you imagine how cool it will be to go to school there? I can't wait."

Angus smiled. "Yeah, it's gonna be great."

Early the next morning, Angus, Vanora, and Mr. Pegenstecher met at the shore and boarded a boat Fane had waiting for them. It was a large vessel, not nearly as big as the Black Mary, but big enough in its own right. The ship bore a large dragonhead on its prow, apparently to frighten away sea monsters and any other evil they might encounter at sea. At the right side of the ship near the back was a large paddle attached to the hull. Angus admired the large steering paddle with its interwoven circles in brilliant, blue knotwork. The body of the ship was pointed at each end and wide in the middle, like a peapod. The hull shone a glossy honey-brown, made up of overlapping planks of wood that were held together by iron rivets.

Mr. Pegenstecher had so much equipment it took nearly half an hour just to load it all.

"I'm so sorry for the holdup," he said. "I promise, it won't be much longer now, and we should be ready to board."

"Are you sure you'll be needing all this?" Fane asked.

Mr. Pegenstecher nodded. "Oh yes, it's very important. Cryptozoology is a science, and like all scientific research, it requires a lot of equipment."

Fane smiled kindly at Mr. Pegenstecher. "Take whatever you like. I'm sure you'll find your research much easier in Ceòban. In fact, I'm confident you will be very busy recording everything you see and hear for days on end."

"Yes, indeed," beamed Mr. Pegenstecher. "This is a fine opportunity, and I'm grateful for your hospitality. I must admit, I am a bit skeptical and anxious at the same time."

"I'm sure you will not be disappointed. The culture is varied and rich, and there are many beings that exist there. I hope you will find an appreciation of the unique cultures with a human heart rather than with a scientific mind."

"Oh yes, I'm sure I will."

Angus sat beside Vanora, suitcases resting under their feet. The misty island of Iona grew smaller and smaller as they traveled away. The heather-clad hillsides blended into specks of lavender and gold. Angus gazed at the historic abbey until the church faded from view. He thought of his grandfather, Duncan MacBain, resting in the peaceful cemetery, and he turned his face away from the others, so they would not see his tears. He hadn't left the island since he first arrived on the shores of Iona, after his grandfather's death. Angus struggled against the overwhelming sense of sadness at leaving the peace he had found there, the small cottage he and his mother had shared, and the beaches they had combed every morning before dawn.

Vanora took Angus' hand. "What do you think they will be teaching us in school?"

"I'm not sure. Hope it's better than regular school."

"I'd love to learn how to fly, wouldn't you?"

"Fly?" Angus frowned. "No, I don't like heights, remember? I think I'd rather stay on the ground."

"Yeah, I guess that wouldn't be much fun for you." Vanora's face brightened. "How about sword fighting? That would be better suited for a king, wouldn't it?"

Angus smiled. "Definitely! And archery, too!"

"There will be many skills to learn and many subjects to challenge you," Fane said. "You will learn a lot there, but it is still school, and you will have to work hard."

They passed a rocky outcropping with several seals basking in the morning sun. Soon, winter would be here, and the seals would be gone as well. The creatures slipped with ease into the water, and Angus' heart twisted. "Wish someone could teach me how to change into a seal like my mother. Then I could go where she goes under the sea."

"Be happy for who you are and what you have, Angus."

Angus looked into Fane's eyes. He had almost lost the old man, and thankfully, here he was, standing before him once again. A wave of guilt washed over Angus. "You're right. I'm lucky to have you, Vanora, and Mr. Pegenstecher. I won't take any of you for granted. I'm glad to be here, to be alive, and to be spending a whole school year together."

"Now that's the attitude to live by. Oh, and by the way, did I tell you about learning to breathe fire?"

Angus stared at Fane in shock. "Breathe fire—really? We could learn to do that?"

"Oh yes, and I don't just mean from eating spicy foods!"

Angus laughed. "That would be pretty cool!"

"And then there's Omnilingualism," Fane said. "That's a fun one."

"Omni—what is that? I can't even pronounce it."

"It's the ability to understand any language. It is quite useful, especially when dealing with western wood sprites. They can be most disagreeable! Always trying to speak in some secret language so they can rob you of your purple mushrooms." The old man's voice filled with excitement. "And controlling the weather… always fun to *literally* rain on someone's parade and all." Fane shook his head. "It brings to mind so many fond childhood memories. You will enjoy it, I'm sure."

Angus smiled at Fane as they sailed beyond the horizon, toward the enchanted world of Ceòban.

The End

About The Author

Angela Townsend was born in the beautiful Rocky Mountains of Missoula, Montana. As a child, Angela grew up listening to stories told by her grandparents, ancient tales and legends of faraway places. Influenced by her Irish and Scottish heritage, Angela became an avid research historian, specializing in Celtic mythology. Her gift for storytelling finally led her to a full time career in historical research and writing. A writer in local community circulations, Angela is also a published genealogical and historical resource writer who has taught numerous research seminars. Currently, Angela divides her time between writing, playing Celtic music on her fiddle, and Irish dancing.

Angela's first novel, Amarok, was published through Spencer Hill Press in 2012. Her newest novel, Angus MacBain and The Island of Sleeping Kings, was signed for publication with Clean Teen Publishing in 2013.

Angela resides on a ranch, in rural Northwestern Montana, with her two children Levi and Grant.

Acknowledgements

I would like to thank everyone at Clean Teen Publishing for making Angus MacBain come alive in print. I would also like to thank my editors, Cindy Davis, Mariah McGarvey and Emily White. I would also like to acknowledge my friends, John Sinrud, David and Alicia Henderson, and Toni Kerr. My godfather, Jim Fitzgerald, and my entire family for their continued love and support.

A very special thank you to my boss, Dale L. McGarvey for his continued support.

In memory of my ancestors from ancient Hibernia and Caledonia--thank you for the gift of storytelling.

CPSIA information can be obtained at www.ICGtesting.com
Printed in the USA
LVOW12s1203311214

421056LV00001B/1/P